THE USBORNE BOOK OF
DRAWING, PAINTING & LETTERING

Susan Mayes, Anna Claybourne, Fiona Watt and Patricia Lovett

Series Editor: Cheryl Evans

Contents

Starting Drawing	2
Starting Painting	33
Starting Lettering	65
Index	96

Designed by Lindy Dark and Vicki Groombridge
Illustrated by Terry Burton, Lindy Dark and Sue Stitt
Photographs by Howard Allman
Art consultant: Gill Figg

Editorial assistant: Rachael Swann

STARTING DRAWING

Contents

2 Things you need

4 Making marks

6 Seeing shapes

8 Taking a line for a walk

10 Shading and blending

12 Magic cubes

14 Near and far

16 Light on dark

18 Fantastic feet

20 Different styles

22 Cartoons

24 Movement, speed and sound

26 Portraits

28 Design and make a mask

30 Out and about

32 Drawings and galleries

Things you need

You don't need much to start drawing. You can draw with any pencil, pen, crayon or chalk on all different kinds of paper. These two pages show you some of the things that will be useful in this part of the book.

Pencils

A pencil is the easiest thing to draw with, and pencils are cheap and easy to find. Pencil leads can be harder or softer. They make different kinds of marks.

Look on the side of the pencil for the label showing the hardness of the lead.

110   2B

H stands for hard and B stands for black. Black pencils are softer. A 6B is a very soft pencil, which you can smudge easily. H pencils are harder and make fainter lines. An HB pencil is in the middle.

2H

HB

2B

6B

The higher the number, the softer or harder the pencil.

Paper

Art and craft stores sell many different kinds of paper in all shades and sizes. Look for paper with interesting textures, such as rough, smooth and shiny.

Smooth white artists' paper often comes in a pad. You can buy different sizes.

Sugar paper has a rough surface and comes in different shades.

Pens and crayons

You can do bright drawings with pencils, crayons, felt-tip pens, chalks or pastels.

Bright pencils are good for detailed drawings and delicate shades.

Pastels or chalks can be smudged and blended together with your finger.

Crayons are bright and bold.

Felt-tip pens are good for filling in spaces.

You can draw on cardboard too. Try the inside of a cereal box.

Some of the projects in this book use tracing paper.

Paper comes in lots of bright shades.

Tissue paper

Extra things

As well as drawing, this book has some exciting projects for you to do. You will need scissors, paper glue, tape and a pencil sharpener. You also need a large, flat table or other space to work on.

Charcoal

Charcoal makes a mark like a very soft, black pencil. It is made from burned twigs. Artists often use it for sketching pictures. You can buy it from art and craft stores.

To smudge charcoal, draw on paper and gently rub the marks with your finger.

Charcoal also comes in pencils.

Charcoal is very messy, so cover pictures with another piece of paper before you put them away.

Other ways to draw

You don't have to use only pens and pencils. Try out some more unusual tools.

Try drawing with a brush and ink or thin paint.

If you go to a sandy beach, you can do huge drawings in the sand with a stick or your finger.

Use a cotton bud and paint to do a simple picture.

Try doing a drawing with a twig dipped in paint or ink.

3

Making marks

You can use pencils, crayons and other drawing tools to make lots of different marks and patterns.

Lines

Lines can be straight or curly, thick or thin, long or short. How many different kinds of lines can you make?

Can you draw a straight line without a ruler?

Try holding a pencil on its side and drawing with the side of the lead.

You can use long lines to make shapes.

Lots of short lines close together can look like fur or grass.

Sharp or hard pencils make thin lines.

Use a blunter or softer pencil for thicker lines.

With soft pencils, chalks or pastels, you can smudge lines with your finger to make them softer.

Dots and spots

Drawing lots of little dots with the tip of a pencil or pen is called pointillism (say *pwant*-ill-ism). You can use it to fill in big spaces.

Try a mixture of dots in different shades. From farther away, the shades blend together.

Rubbing patterns

Making rubbings is a good way to make marks. Find things that have rough patterns, or textures, on them, such as wooden things, keys or leaves.

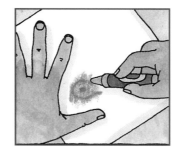

To make a rubbing, hold a piece of paper still over the thing and rub up and down over it with a crayon or soft pencil.

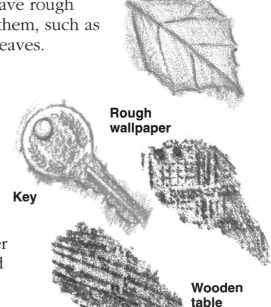

Leaf

Rough wallpaper

Key

Wooden table

Big-leaved tree picture

You can use different kinds of drawing marks to make whole pictures.

You will need:
Pencils, crayons or pastels
Thin, smooth paper in different shades
Rough brown or green paper or cardboard
Scissors and glue
Small leaves

1

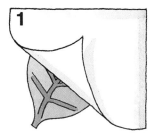

Turn a leaf over to show the ridges on the back. Lay some white paper on top and hold it still.

2

Using the edge of a pencil or crayon, rub gently up and down on the paper all over the leaf.

3
Make leaves of different shades and sizes.

Carefully cut around the outline of the leaf. Make more leaves in the same way.

4

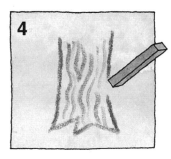

For a tree trunk, draw thick, wavy green and brown lines on the rough paper or cardboard.

5

Overlap the leaves.

Cut the trunk out and glue it onto a large piece of paper. Then glue the leaves around the top.

You could make rubbings from other things, and then cut out leaf shapes from them.

You could show a leaf falling off the tree.

Draw short green lines to make grass.

Seeing shapes

Everything you can see is made up of shapes. These pages show you how to look for shapes and draw outlines.

Air drawing

Before you draw something, look at its shape carefully. Close one eye, reach out, and "draw" around the object in the air with your finger. This is called air drawing. It helps you see what shape things are.

Some things, such as a bottle, have a simple shape.

Some things have a complicated shape, like this leafy plant.

Drawing outlines

1

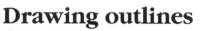

Start with a simple shape.

Choose something to draw. Place it a short distance away from you. Look carefully at its shape.

2

Try air drawing the thing (see above) to help you see exactly what shape it is.

3

Now use a pencil to draw the outline on your paper. Don't draw the details inside the shape.

Try something with a more complicated outline.

4

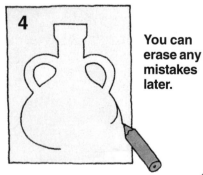

You can erase any mistakes later.

If it looks wrong, just draw a new line where you want it and leave the old one there.

Look around for things that have interesting shapes.

Shape collage

A collage is a picture made from lots of different shapes glued onto paper. Try making a collage from shapes you have drawn.

You will need:
A pencil
Paper of different shades, textures and thicknesses
Scissors and glue

Can you tell what all these shapes are?

Tissue paper

You can make the shapes overlap.

1

Choose a collection of things to draw. You could just use things from the kitchen, for example.

2

Using a pencil, draw outlines of all the things on different kinds of paper.

3

If you like, you could add dots, lines or other patterns, like the ones on page 4, to your shapes.

4

Carefully cut out the shapes and arrange them on a large piece of paper. Glue them down.

Pattern of dots made with a felt-tip pen

Shiny paper

Taking a line for a walk

Most things are made up of lots of shapes. Here's an interesting way to put all the shapes together. You move smoothly from one part of your picture to another without taking your pen off the paper. This is called taking a line for a walk.

You will need:
A felt-tip pen and some paper
Something to draw, such as a shoe, a flower or a person

Start drawing

1

You could use a photograph.

Begin by looking carefully at the thing you are going to draw. What shapes can you see?

2

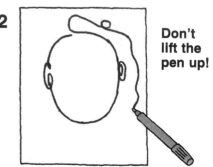

Don't lift the pen up!

Put your pen on the paper to start your drawing. It is easiest to start with the outline of your picture.

3

Make your line curve and twist to include the main shapes. You don't have to draw every detail.

You can go over the same line twice.

You may have to do a line where you can't really see one. In this picture, for example, there is a line from the hair to the eyebrow.

Use your line to do squiggles, shading in, or other patterns along the way.

8

Abstract line walk

An abstract drawing is a drawing that isn't a picture of anything. Sometimes it's just lots of shapes. You can make an abstract drawing by taking a line for a walk all over a piece of paper.

Draw a long line that curves, twists, zigzags or crosses over itself to make lots of patterns. Fill in the spaces in different shades.

You could fill in the spaces with patterns (see page 4).

Try an abstract line walk using just straight lines.

Mounting

Mounting a picture on a bright background gives it a border, which looks good when you display your work.

You will need:
Paper or cardboard
Scissors and glue
Pencil and ruler

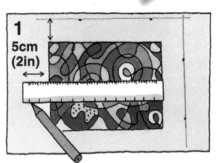

1
5cm (2in)

Measure a piece of paper or cardboard 5cm (2in) wider and 5cm (2in) taller than the picture on each side.

2

Cut out the cardboard or paper mount and glue your picture neatly in the middle of it.

9

Shading and blending

Shading means filling in the dark and light areas in your drawings. It makes things look solid and real. The darkness or lightness of a mark is called the tone. Harder and softer pencils make different tones (see page 2).

Dark to light

1 Sharpen the pencil if it gets blunt.

To make a very dark tone, press hard with your pencil. Go over the same part again and again.

2

Try to keep the tone even.

To make lighter tones, hold the pencil on its side, press gently, and shade back and forth.

3

Try different shades using bright pencils.

Try changing tone gradually along in a strip on the paper. Press less and less hard as you go.

Find out how to draw these zooming rockets below.

Zooming rockets

Soft drawing tools like charcoal and pastels are easy to smudge and blend. Use them to draw a whoosh of rocket flames.

You will need:
A large piece of paper
Felt-tip pens or crayons
Pastels, chalks or charcoal

1 You could draw the rockets with felt-tips or crayons.

Draw some flying rockets. Shade them in if you want to.

2

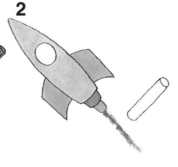

Draw thick charcoal or pastel lines coming from the rockets.

3 Use a quick, sweeping movement.

Use a finger to rub the flames away from the rocket.

10

A shaded drawing

Choose something round and simple to draw, like a ball or some fruit.

You will need:
White paper
Whatever you want to draw with, such as a pencil, charcoal or pastels
A spotlight

1

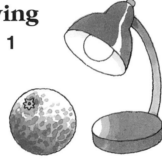

Place your object under the light. Switch off any other lights and close the curtains if possible.

2

Highlight

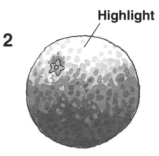

Look at the dark and light parts. The brightest part, where the light reflects, is called the highlight.

3

Try moving the light around to see how the dark and light parts change. Does the highlight move?

4

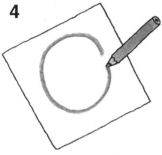

When you are happy with how the object looks, start drawing. Begin with the outline of the shape.

5

Shade in the darker parts of the drawing first, then the lighter ones. For a highlight, leave white paper.

Charcoal drawing

Pastel drawing

Try drawing the same thing using different tools or shades.

The different tones in something show its shape.

The highlight is in the middle of this orange.

Lighter area

Dark area

11

Magic cubes

There is a simple secret to drawing a cube. Once you know it, you can use cubes in lots of different ways to make pictures.

1

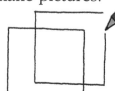

Start by drawing a square on a piece of paper with a pencil. This will be the front of your cube.

2

Now draw another square that is slightly smaller. Make it overlap the first square, like this.

3

a

b

Now join the corners of the squares with lines (shown in blue). You have drawn a see-through cube.

4

To make the cube look solid, erase the three lines inside the cube (shown here in red).

What can a cube be?

A cube can be a box, or it can be all kinds of other things. Just add details.

Draw ribbons and bright patterns for a present.

For a fishtank, draw a see-through cube. Add some water and fish.

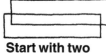

Add a screen and buttons to make a television.

You can make long boxes, or cuboids, the same way.

Start with two oblong shapes.

Join the corners together.

For a bus or train, draw a long oblong box. Add wheels and windows.

Light and shade

When light shines at a cube, the side nearest the light looks brightest. The other sides are in the shade, so they look darker. Try shading in your cubes like this.

Imagine a light shining from the right.

This side would be the lightest.

This side would be the darkest, if you could see it.

The other sides would be a medium shade.

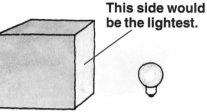

Imagine a light on the left of a cube.

This side would be very dark.

You can't see the bright side.

These sides would be a medium shade.

Can you shade a cube with the light coming from other sides?

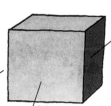

Cube robot

You can create a robot using cube and box shapes. Decorate it with eyes, feelers, controls, flashing lights, wheels or other robot parts.

You will need:
A large piece of paper
A pencil
Felt-tip pens, wax crayons or pencil crayons for shading in

1

Erase any lines you don't want as you go.

Draw big cube shapes one above the other for the robot's head, body and base.

2

Join the three parts of the robot together with wiggly wires, using a felt-tip pen or crayon.

3

Add arms, eyes, buttons, dials and any other parts you like.

4

Imagine the light is in the same place for each cube.

Shade in the cubes in different tones so that they look solid.

This side of the robot is turned away from you, so you can't see as much of the arm and ear.

This side of the robot looks nearer to you.

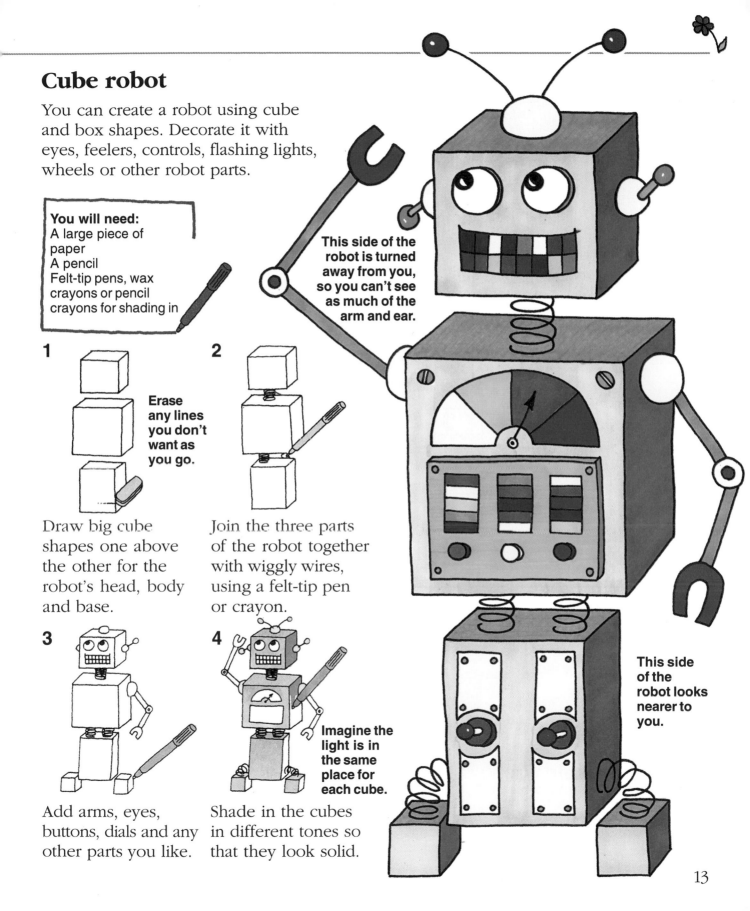

13

Near and far

Things that are near to you look much bigger than things that are far away. When you are doing a drawing, you can make some of the things in it look nearer to you by drawing them larger. To see for yourself how near things look bigger than faraway things, try the experiment below.

Foreground and background

The word foreground is used to describe things that look very near in a picture. Things that are far away are in the background.

In this picture, the ducks are in the foreground and the trees are in the background.

See for yourself

1

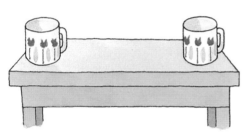

Find two things that are about the same size as each other. Place them far apart on a table, like this.

2

Stand at one end of the table. Bend down so that your eyes are level with the two things. Cover one eye.

3

Look at the two things carefully. Do they look different sizes? You could try drawing them.

Near and far landscape picture

Make a picture showing near and faraway things, using tracing paper. A landscape or outdoor picture works best.

You will need:
2 sheets of tracing paper
1 sheet of white paper the same size as the tracing paper
Felt-tips or crayons
Clear tape

1

Draw near the top of the paper.

Start by drawing the background on the white paper. Draw some hills, sky and small trees.

2

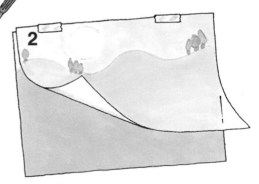

Lay a piece of tracing paper neatly over the picture. Fasten them together at the top with tape.

The three layers make it seem as if you are looking into the distance.

The tracing paper makes the faraway things look fainter, as they do in real life.

3

Make the nearer trees bigger than the faraway ones.

4

5

Draw some more things on the tracing paper. Make these things bigger so that they look nearer.

Now lay the second sheet of tracing paper over the drawing. Fasten it to the drawing at the top.

On the top sheet, draw the things in the foreground. These should be the biggest things in the picture.

Light on dark

In the dark, lights from buildings, machines and fires glow. Sometimes you can't even see the shapes of things, only the lights shining from them. Here are some ways to draw lights at night. Try using black, dark blue or purple paper and bright pastels or chalks.

Light effects

Streetlights glow like this.

You don't need to draw the outline of the building.

For a glowing light, draw a dot or square. Rub it with a finger to make it look as if it is glowing.

Draw rows of windows with a yellow chalk on black paper. They look like a skyscraper at night.

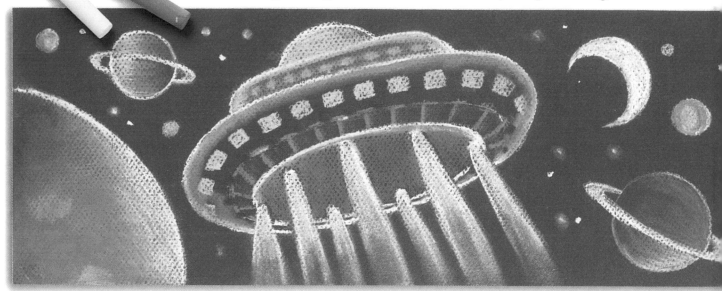

The sky at night

Using pastels or chalks, try drawing a space scene with planets and brightly lit-up spacecraft. Add stars and moons for a night sky.

You will need:
A big, long piece of black or dark blue paper
Pastels or chalks in different shades

1

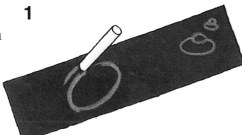

For spacecraft, draw large oval, sausage or rocket shapes on the paper.

2 Rub the lights to make them glow.

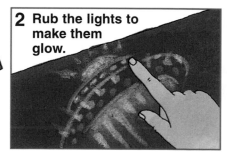

Add rows of windows, glowing lights or light beams to the spacecraft.

A lighthouse or a car's headlights send out beams.

Draw spots of light in yellow pastel or chalk. Rub away from the spot to make a light beam.

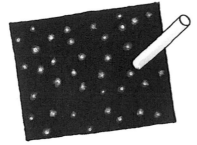

For stars at night, do lots of tiny white dots. Lots of yellow dots look like the lights of a town or city.

Scratch drawings

To make drawings like these, cover a piece of giftwrap or a page from a magazine with thick, black crayon.

Use a spoon or paintbrush handle to scratch a picture. The bright paper will show through the black crayon.

Try drawing fireworks or a city.

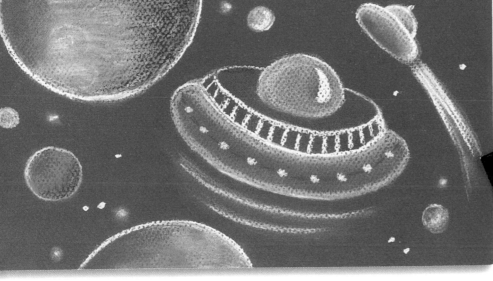

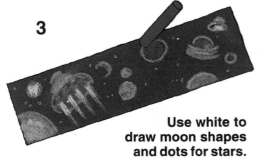

3

Use white to draw moon shapes and dots for stars.

For planets, draw circles and shade them in. You could add spots or patterns.

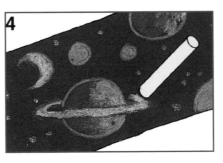

4

For a ring around a planet, draw a long oval, half in front of the planet and half behind.

Fantastic feet

Drawing people from real life is called life drawing. Drawing a whole person can be hard, but you could try just drawing your feet, to see what it's like.

You will need:
Plain white paper
A board or large book to rest on
A pencil, charcoal, or whatever you want to draw with
Two chairs (one to sit on, one to rest your feet on)

Feet from life

1 **Hold your paper on your lap.**

Sit with your feet resting on a chair. Make sure you are comfortable, so you won't have to move around.

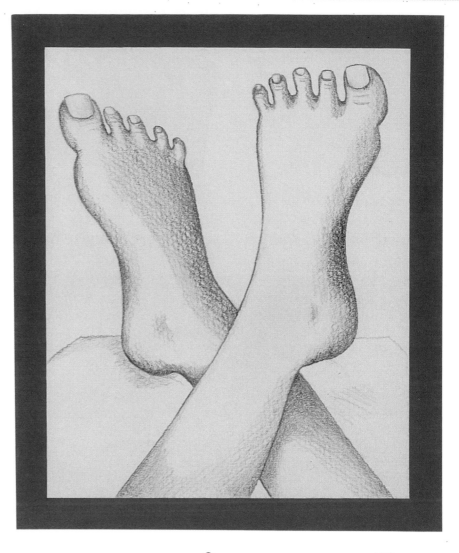

2 Start with the outline. Look carefully at the shapes you can see. You could try "air drawing" (see page 6) first.

3 Add details of any other shapes and lines you can see, such as toenails, freckles or tiny wrinkles.

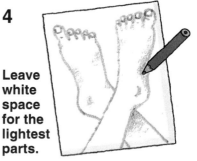

4 **Leave white space for the lightest parts.**

Can you see darker and lighter areas on your feet? See if you can shade them in on your drawing.

Still life shoes

Drawing things that do not move is called still life. It's easiest if you start with just one thing. Here's an idea for drawing a still life picture (see page 50).

1

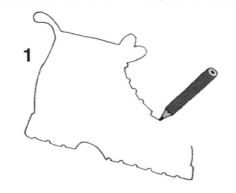

Draw the outline of the shoe. Try to include all the details around the outline, like laces and bumpy soles.

2

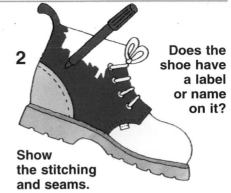

Does the shoe have a label or name on it?

Show the stitching and seams.

Add details such as buckles, laces, stitching or patterns. Shade in or decorate the shoe with pens or crayons.

If you can see inside the shoe, draw that part too.

To cut out a hole, poke your scissors through first.

Shoe bookmarks

Cut out the hard parts, like laces, at the end.

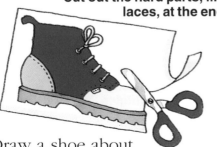

Draw a shoe about 10cm (4in) long on thin cardboard. Carefully cut it out to make a bookmark.

To make the bookmarks last longer, you could cover them with book-covering plastic.

Different styles

You don't always have to draw in the same way. Artists often have their own way of drawing, or style, which they like to use. Here are some different styles of drawing for you to try.

Collage

Try mixing collage (see page 7) with drawing to make pictures.

You will need:
Scissors
Glue stick
A thick felt-tip pen
Paper in different shades

1

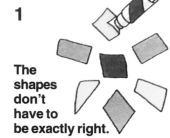

The shapes don't have to be exactly right.

Cut simple petal shapes out of bright paper. Glue them down to make a flower shape.

2

Use simple, bold lines.

With a thick pen, draw the shape of the flower over the top of the paper pieces.

Black and white

You can do bold, striking pictures using just a black pen.

Try flowers with bold patterns, stripes and spots.

Shade part of a flower with black lines drawn close together. This is called hatching.

For darker shading draw two sets of lines that cross over each other. This is called cross-hatching.

Stained glass window

Stained glass is often used in church windows. It is made of bright pieces of glass fitted together like a jigsaw.

1

First, use a thick black felt-tip pen to draw a flower shape on a piece of paper.

2

Use bright, strong shades.

Draw curved lines across parts of the picture to divide it into smaller spaces. Shade them in.

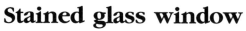

Geometric

Shapes like triangles, circles and rectangles are geometric shapes. You can use them to make pictures.

You will need:
Felt-tip pens or colored pencils
A coin to draw around
Plain paper
A ruler

For a flower with diamond petals, do a circle first. Draw six lines evenly spaced around the circle.

Use a ruler if you want.

Add a triangle shape on each side of each line to make the diamond petals. Then shade them in.

Make sure all the circles fit together closely.

For a flower made of circles, draw around a coin. Put one circle in the middle and the rest around it.

Try drawing a bunch of flowers in different styles.

You can use any style for the ribbon.

21

Cartoons

Cartoons are simple, funny drawings that often tell a story. Here are some ways to show different moods and feelings on cartoon faces.

Here's an ordinary cartoon face.

Different kinds of eyebrows, mixed with mouth shapes, change the mood on a cartoon face.

V-shaped eyebrows with a straight mouth look very angry.

The mouth is very important. It can make faces look sad, happy or surprised.

Smiling mouth

Sad mouth

A wiggly line makes a face look scared.

Change the eyes too.

Laughing mouth

A round mouth looks surprised.

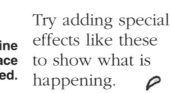

Try sloping eyebrows with a sad mouth.

V-shaped eyebrows and a smiley mouth look naughty.

Try adding special effects like these to show what is happening.

Add drops of sweat for a very hot, tired person.

Add crossed eyes.

Stars or a swirly cloud around the head make a person look dizzy.

Moving bodies

Here's how to add bodies to your cartoon faces.

Erase the stick body later.

Draw a stick body, then add clothes and shoes on top.

Always draw the stick body first, then add clothes.

For a running person, show legs and arms bent like this.

Different clothes show different jobs or hobbies.

For jumping, put the arms behind the body and the legs in front.

What other things can you make stick people do?

Cartoon animals

For cartoon animals, think about the main shapes that help you recognize an animal. For example, a cat has big ears and whiskers.

Draw the mouth like a big "w."

Draw funny eyebrows to give the cat a mood.

Sometimes cartoons make animals look like people. Try a cat's face with human clothes.

A pig is fat with a round snout and curly tail.

A mouse has a pointed nose and a long tail.

Here are some more cartoon animals to try. Give them funny cartoon faces to show different moods.

Jungle scene

You can also draw cartoon scenes, like this cartoon jungle. Remember, you can put anything you like in a cartoon, even if it wouldn't happen in real life.

A giraffe has a long neck and legs.

A hippo has a fat body with stumpy legs and a long, bumpy head.

Tiger

A monkey has a big nose, big ears and a long tail.

For jungle leaves, draw long triangle shapes.

Birds have egg-shaped bodies. Their necks can be long or short.

Mane

A crocodile has a long lumpy body.

This lion has a triangle head and a big furry mane.

Draw big, bright jungle flowers.

A snake is a wiggly shape with a round head.

Movement, speed and sound

Here are some tricks for making your cartoons look as if they are moving, and for showing noises and exciting actions.

Zoom lines

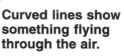

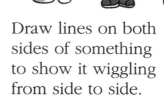

Draw a few straight lines behind something to show it speeding along.

For something really fast, add a cloud of dust around the lines, like this.

Draw lines on both sides of something to show it wiggling from side to side.

Splat! Boom!

In cartoons, you can show noises by drawing a word with a shape around it. Try words like Kapow! Boom! Boinggg! Splash! and Splat!

SPLAT!

Draw a puddle shape and water drops for a wet, sticky splat.

Big zigzags around a word show a loud noise or explosion.

BOOM!

Use bright red and yellow for an explosion.

KAPOW!

Draw a big flash like this to show a loud bang or crash.

The flash is made up of a circle of U shapes.

Speech bubbles

HEY! COME BACK!

HEY! COME BACK!

Write words in clear letters near the cartoon's head.

Draw an oval bubble around the words, with a small pointer.

YUM YUM!

Draw a trail of smaller bubbles leading to the thinker.

To show thoughts, do the words in a cloud-shaped bubble.

MEET ME AT HQ...

Do zigzag bubbles for a telephone or loudspeaker sound.

Animated flick book

Animated pictures look as if they are moving when you see them quickly one after another. Here you can make a flick book showing a flower opening. Flick through the pictures in the top corner of pages 2 to 32 to see how it works.

Flick this book like this.

You will need:
A small notebook with plenty of pages
Pens or pencils
Scissors and glue

When you have finished, flick through the book like this to watch the animated cartoon.

You could draw a cover picture for your flick book on a piece of paper, and glue it to the front.

1

Leave some space around the flower. **Use this edge.**

On the first page of the book, draw a small flower like this.

2

Put the flower in the same place.

On the next page, draw a slightly bigger flower.

3

Draw in the same place on each page.

Gradually make the flower petals grow bigger and bigger.

4

Shade the flower in, if you like.

Make the flower open out until it is as big as it can be.

More ideas

Here are some more animation ideas. Do each picture on a new page. (You will need to do more pictures than are shown here.)

Make this man walk along the page until he slips.

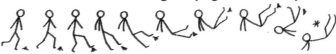

Make the bird fly across the page.

Make the frog jump up and down.

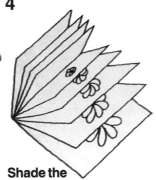

Portraits

A portrait is a drawing of a person. Artists usually draw portraits from real life, but you can copy from a photograph. You could even draw a self-portrait by sitting in front of a mirror.

Faces and features

Parts of people's faces, like eyes, noses and mouths, are called features. Look at how people's features are arranged on their faces. It helps if you think of the head as an oval with four parts.

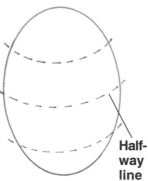

Half-way line

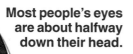

Most people's eyes are about halfway down their head.

The ears are usually level with the eyes.

The nose and mouth are just under the eyes, about three-quarters of the way down.

Hair usually fills up the top quarter of the head and is longer at the sides.

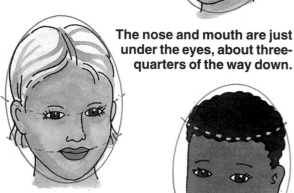

Drawing a portrait

The person you draw is called the sitter. Make sure she is comfortable. She will have to sit still for about 20 minutes.

You will need:
A piece of paper
Pencils
Something to rest on, like a large book
An eraser

1

You can erase any wrong lines later.

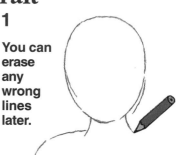

Lightly draw the main shapes. Most portraits show just the head and shoulders.

2

Use the shapes you have drawn to help you draw a stronger, more careful outline.

3

How big are your sitter's eyes, and where are they? Draw them next.

4

Shade in dark areas, like eyes and nostrils.

Add eyebrows and work on down the face. Look at the nose and draw that next.

5

Are there lines from the nose to the mouth?

Now draw the mouth, and any other things, like glasses or earrings.

26

6

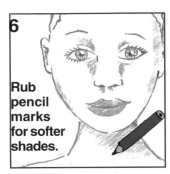

Rub pencil marks for softer shades.

Are there shadows under the chin or around the eyes or nose? Shade them in.

7

Use lines that follow the way the hair grows.

Draw in the sitter's hair and clothes. Try to copy any patterns like stripes or spots.

Stand-up mount

Here's how to make a stand-up mount to display your portraits. First, mount the portrait on cardboard, as shown on page 9.

You will need:
Cardboard
A pencil and ruler
Scissors and tape
Glue

Try making a mini-portrait.

You could draw a background too.

You could decorate the frame with felt-tip pens.

1 Fold over about 2cm (1in) from the end.

Cut a piece of cardboard that is smaller than your mount. Fold the end over.

2 Now you can stand the frame up.

Tape the folded-over part to the back of your frame, about halfway up.

Portraits long ago

Before photographs were invented, rich people often used to pay to have their portraits drawn or painted.

27

Design and make a mask

Sometimes it's easier to make things if you think about what you want them to look like and draw them first. This is called designing. These pages show you how to design a mask on paper, and then make it using cardboard.

Designing

1

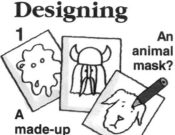

An animal mask?

A made-up mask?

First, decide what kind of mask you want to make. Try drawing some of your ideas on paper.

2

What shape should it be?

Could you glue things onto it?

Think about how you could make the mask look the way you want it to. There are some ideas below.

3

Keep trying out ideas until you decide on a design you want. Now you can make a pattern for a mask.

4

Leave lots of space around the oval.

On a new piece of paper, draw an oval base shape about 20cm (8in) tall and 15cm (6in) wide.

5

Change and correct it as much as you like.

Now draw the shape you want your mask to be, around the base shape. This is your mask pattern.

6

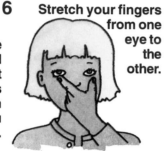

Stretch your fingers from one eye to the other.

You will need to see out of eyes in the mask. Use your hand to measure how far apart your eyes are.

7

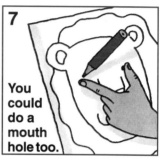

You could do a mouth hole too.

Use your stretched fingers to mark two eye spots halfway up the oval. Draw eye holes around them.

Design ideas

Think about ways to make your masks look exciting.

How could you make a furry animal mask?

You could glue on pieces of yarn or wool.

Spiky edges look like fur.

What would make it look like a robot?

Foil or silver paper looks like metal.

You could glue on small metal things, such as paper clips.

What could you do to make it look like a person?

You could cut a hat shape out of cloth.

Moustache and beard made of crepe paper.

Making your mask

Now you can use your design to help you make the finished mask out of cardboard.

You will need:
Thin cardboard
Pencil, scissors, tape
Pens or crayons
Glue and things to glue to the mask

1

Carefully cut out your paper pattern. Cut holes for the eyes, and a mouth hole if you want one.

2

Draw any holes too.

Lay the paper design on the cardboard. Tape it down and draw around it carefully with a pencil.

3

Cut out the mask. Ask for help with the holes. Decorate the mask so it looks the way you want it to.

4

The strips should be level with the eyeholes.

Cut two cardboard strips 30cm (12in) long, 2cm (1in) wide. Tape them to the back of the mask like this.

5

Overlap the strips around your head. Tape them together at the right length to hold the mask on.

Yarn and strips of paper glued on as a mane.

This queen mask has yellow yarn hair and gumdrop jewels.

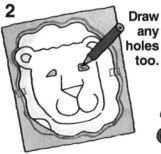

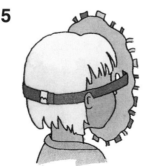

Out and about

Drawings are all around you wherever you go. See how many different drawing styles you can find on everyday things.

Pictures in books are called illustrations.

Look for drawings on boxes and wrappings.

You can find cartoons in comics and newspapers.

Even a map is a kind of drawing.

Cartoons on television are made up of lots of drawings, like the flick books on page 25.

Keeping a sketchbook

A sketchbook is perfect for drawing in when you go out. You can also cut out other drawings and glue them in.

A book with plain pages and a hard cover is best. You can buy one at a card shop or art store.

Try drawing things that catch your eye, wherever you are. Take your sketchbook on holiday or on a walk.

You could draw flowers or trees.

You could draw whole buildings, or just look at one detail.

Glue drawings from old magazines and boxes into your book.

If you can't cut a picture out, you could try copying it.

You can learn how to make your own sketchbook on page 56.

Going to galleries

Art galleries have both drawings and paintings for people to look at and enjoy. Galleries in large towns are often free to go in. If you go to a gallery, look out for drawings.

Galleries often sell postcards with their pictures on them.

Take your sketchbook and copy some of the pictures you like.

Some artists do small drawings before they do a painting. Sometimes you can see these next to paintings.

Artists and their styles

These drawings are done in the styles of some famous artists. You might see their drawings in a gallery.

Leonardo da Vinci (1452-1519) was an artist, scientist and inventor. He did detailed drawings of people, animals and machines.

Henri Matisse (1869-1954) experimented with bold lines in bright shades. He often drew with a brush and ink or paint.

Henry Moore (1898-1986) did rounded drawings of people and animals. He made sculptures and statues in the same style.

M.C. Escher (1898-1970) is famous for his clever pencil drawings of animals, birds and other shapes that fit together.

Paul Klee (1879-1940) drew and painted many buildings and landscapes. He liked to use patterns made up of lots of simple shapes.

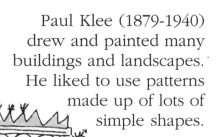

Drawings and galleries

Many famous artists drew as well as painted. Here you can learn about their drawings. Sometimes they used them to help make a finished painting. You could look for their drawings in books in your local library.

Edgar Degas (1848-1903)

Degas was very skilled at drawing. He drew from memory a lot and used his drawings to help with his paintings. He would scribble down a face he had seen, or might work for months on a life drawing. (See page 18). He liked to use pastel best. The *Jeu de Paume gallery in Paris* has lots of his art.

John Constable (1776-1837)

He is best known for his landscape paintings of Suffolk in England. He used his drawings as 'notes' for his larger paintings. These are very tiny pictures of buildings, trees, people and clouds in the sky. You can see his drawings in the *Victoria and Albert Museum in London, England.*

David Hockney (b. 1937)

Hockney's line drawings are very clever. He draws straight onto the paper with a stylo tip pen. This makes a very fine line. There is a museum of his work in *Bradford, England.*

Frederick Leighton (1830-1896)

He is famous for painting, sculpture and drawing. He made drawings of people before painting them. Some people like his drawings better than his paintings. The *Royal Academy, in London, England,* has many of his drawings.

Leonardo da Vinci (1452-1519)

Da Vinci had amazing notebooks, filled with drawings. He did lots of sketches before starting a painting to see where things should go. He used red chalk, pen and silverpoint. This is a silver wire which makes very fine lines. The best collection of his drawings is at *Windsor Castle in England.*

L. S. Lowry (1887-1976)

Lowry filled his notebooks with drawings of streets. He used them later for his paintings. He was interested in buildings and used criss-cross strokes for dark shading. (See page 20). For his art gallery turn to page 64.

Pablo Picasso (1881-1973)

Picasso could draw as well as any artist when he was still very young. He spent the rest of his long life trying to draw in a simpler style. He also used different shapes to make collages. (See page 7). One is made of newspaper, letters and has a drawing of a guitar in the background. You can see his work in *American, French and Spanish galleries.*

Rembrandt (1606-1669)

He is a very famous Dutch artist. Most of his drawings were made from the things he saw around him. He often used a thick reed pen. With a few quick marks he could draw a face. His work can be seen in the *National Gallery, London, the Rijkmuseum, Amsterdam and other European galleries.*

Georges Seurat (1859-1891)

Seurat's drawings were an important part of his work. He learned that the directions of lines could show different feelings. Upward slanting lines are happy, straight lines are calm and downward sloping lines are sad. You can find out where to see his paintings on page 64.

STARTING
PAINTING

Contents

34 Things you need

36 Experimenting

38 Making new colors

40 Color blends

42 Color-blend painting

44 Thick paint

46 Color-match spirals

48 Look, paint and print

50 Still life

52 Painting people

54 Sponge and spatter

56 Painting outdoors

58 Paint and stick

60 Computer paintings

62 Artists and paintings

64 More paintings

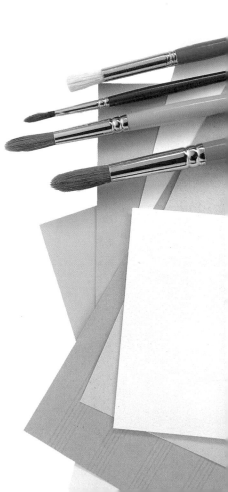

Things you need

This part of the book shows you how to use paint in lots of ways. There are plenty of ideas for things to paint and make using the new skills you learn. On these pages you can see the things you need. Buy them from an arts and crafts or art supply store.

Paints

There are different kinds of paints. The best ones to use for the projects in this book are ready-mixed paint, powder paint or acrylic paint.

Ready-mixed paint

Powder paint

Acrylic paint

Watercolor paints, oil paints and blocks of paint are not good for the projects in this part of the book.

Colors

You need a red, a blue, a yellow, white and black. You may have different reds, blues and yellows to choose from. Pick a red called crimson if you have a choice.

If you like, buy an extra red, blue or yellow.

Thickener

You can make paint thicker by mixing in a thickener such as white glue. Add a little to powder paints or liquid paints. (See page 44.)

Glue looks white until you mix it in.

Don't get any on your clothes as it is difficult to get out.

What to paint on

You may like to buy new paper to use. It comes in different sizes. You need letter or ledger size for most of the things in this book.

You could buy bigger pieces and cut them to the size you need.

Ledger size is 11 x 14 inches

Letter size is 8½ x 11 inches

You can use white or colored paper.

Sketchbook

A sketchbook has blank pages that you can paint, draw or stick on. It is useful for testing colors and trying out ideas.

Find out how to make your own sketchbook on pages 56 and 57.

Brushes

Brushes come in different sizes. Some have soft bristles and some have stiff bristles. It is best to have three soft brushes, for different kinds of painting.

Medium-thickness

Thin, for delicate work

A medium-thickness stiff brush is useful, too.

Thick, for painting big areas

Extra things

You need these extra things every time you paint.

Short plastic pots or a plastic palette, to put paint in

A short jar and a flat plate

Newspaper

Paper towel or a rag

An old shirt or an apron

Before you start

Clear a big space and spread out lots of newspaper.

Collect the things in the list at the beginning of the project and the things shown above.

Put your painting shirt on and fill the jar with clean water.

Make a folder

You could make a folder to put your paintings in. Stick two big sheets of cardboard together with tape. Use sheets that are bigger than ledger size.

You could decorate the folder.

35

Experimenting

You can paint with brushes, but you can use other things too. Collect at least ten different tools that you could paint marks with. Here are some ideas.

Preparing paint

Different kinds of paint need to be prepared in different ways to make them a good thickness for painting with.

Powder paint is dry until you add water to it.

Ready-mixed paint comes ready to use. So does acrylic paint in tubs or bottles.

Acrylic paint in tubes is fairly thick.

Don't fill the pot.

To use ready-mixed paint or acrylic paint in tubs or bottles, just put the color you need in its own pot.

Always put the paint in before the water.

Use a dry spoon

To use powder paint, spoon some into a pot. Drip a few drops of clean water on from a brush. Mix it all in.

Always use clean water for mixing.

To use acrylic paint in tubes, squeeze some into a pot. Mix in drops of water to make the paint creamy.

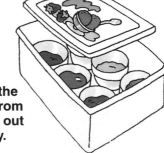

A lid stops the paint from drying out quickly.

If you have some paint left over when you finish painting, put the pots in a plastic tub with a lid on.

Making marks

Things you need:
Three colors of paint
A big sheet of paper
A collection of tools
for making marks
A plate

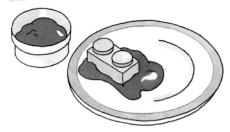

Prepare a color. Put some
on the plate with a brush,
then dip a tool in.

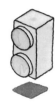

See how many ways you
can use the tool to paint
marks on the paper.

**Brush paint
onto big tools.**

Change the color you use
each time you choose a
new tool.

**Use different
parts of
each tool.**

**You could
write the
name of the
thing you used
beside each mark.**

**Which tool
makes the biggest
number of
different marks?**

Cleaning tips

Always change the water
in the jar if it gets dirty
while you are painting.

Clean each tool when
you have finished
making marks with it.

Wash everything up at the
end, to get the paint off.

37

Making new colors

Red, yellow and blue are called primary colors. You can mix them in different ways to make new colors.

Things you need:
White paper
A pencil and a ruler
Thin wax crayons
(not chunky ones)
Paints
A thin brush
Scissors

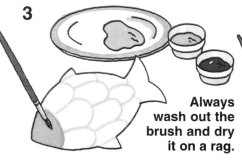

1

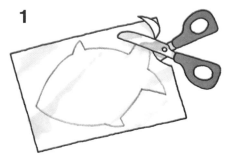

Draw a fat fish shape on the paper and cut it out. Make the fish about 20cm (8in) long.

2

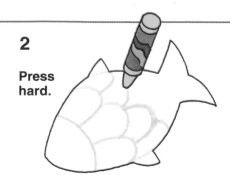

Press hard.

Draw a pattern on the fish with a yellow wax crayon. The pattern needs about 14 shapes in it.

3

Always wash out the brush and dry it on a rag.

Prepare red and yellow paint in pots. Use a brush to put some yellow on a plate. Paint one shape on the fish.

4

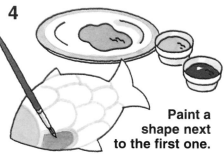

Paint a shape next to the first one.

Add a little red to the yellow on the plate. Mix the colors together. Paint a shape with the new color.

5

Put extra paint on the plate if you run out.

Add a little more red to the color you mixed to change it again. Paint a new shape. Keep making new colors.

Powder paint

Dry powder paint in pots

If the powder won't disappear, add a tiny drop of water.

Dip a damp brush in the yellow powder. Mix it around on the plate. Wash and dry the brush. Then mix in some red.

If you can't make any more colors and your fish has empty spaces, try mixing colors to match ones you have made already.

Can you make a different color for each shape?

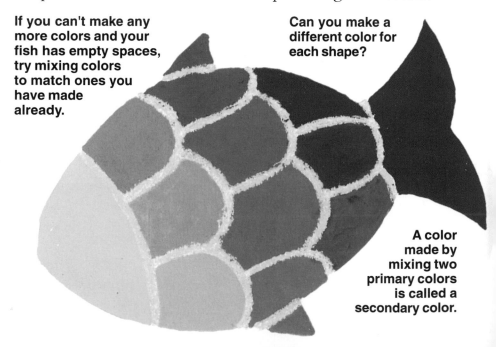

A color made by mixing two primary colors is called a secondary color.

More colors

Use a blue crayon to draw a pattern on another fish. Mix yellow and blue to make lots of new colors.

Add small amounts of blue to yellow.

Cut out a new fish. Draw a pattern with a blue crayon. Mix red and blue to make as many colors as you can.

Start with red, then add blue to it.

Make about 14 spaces.

Use a black crayon to draw a pattern on another fish. Add tiny amounts of black to white and paint the shapes.

Add black to white.

Three-color mix

You can mix yellow, blue and red to make brown. Start with yellow and add small amounts of red and blue. What happens if you add more of one color than another?

This brown has more blue in it.

This brown has more red in it.

This brown has more yellow in it.

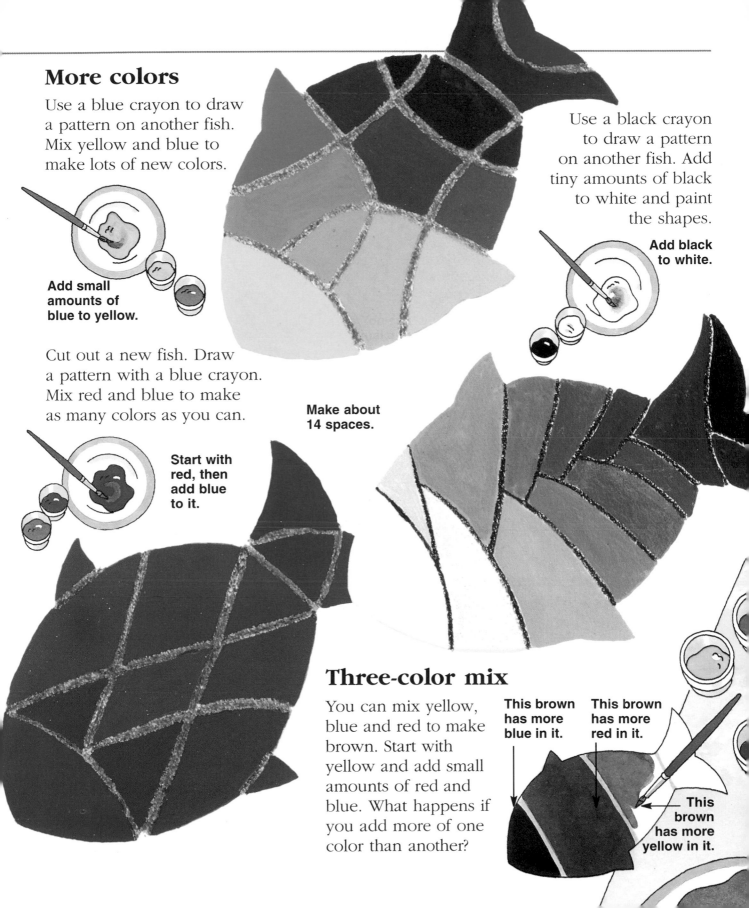

Color blends

Painting colors so they mix into each other is called blending. The picture below has a blended background.

On these pages you need:
Letter size white paper
Paints
Thick and thin soft brushes
A big potato
A scrap of cardboard
Scissors
A rag or paper towel

Dark to light

Thick brush

Paint all the way across.

Prepare blue and white in pots. If you use powder paint, add water to it. Put some of the blue on a plate.

Lay the paper with its short edges at the sides. Paint a blue band across the top. Clean the brush in water.

Work quickly before the paint dries.

Brush the joint to make it disappear.

The lightness or darkness of a color is called its tone.

Mix some white into the blue on the plate, to make it lighter. Paint a band slightly overlapping the first one.

Mix more white into the blue and paint another band. Make each band lighter than the last one, until you finish.

Primary blends

Yellow and red blend

Red and blue blend

Yellow and blue blend

Blend primary colors by following the steps on the left. Use two colors instead of blue and white.

Sailing boats

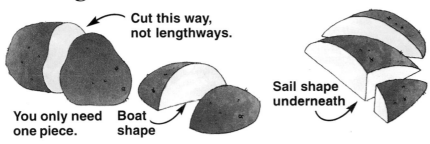

Cut this way, not lengthways.

You only need one piece.

Boat shape

Sail shape underneath

Cut a potato in half. Put one half with its cut side facing down. Cut it in half again. Ask an adult to help.

Take the piece left over from the boat shape. Cut a piece off the bottom. Cut off the curved side.

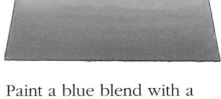

Paint a blue blend with a thick brush. Then turn the paper the other way around and leave it to dry.

Overlap some boats.

Mix a color for the boats. Paint the boat shape and press it onto the paper. Do lots of boats like this.

Wipe the shape before using a new color.

Print a colored sail on each boat. Start on the boats at the top, then work your way down the paper.

Thin brush

Fold a strip of cardboard lengthways. Dip the end in white paint and print waves. Paint lines on the boats.

41

Color-blend painting

You can do lots of different color blends in a painting. Blend pairs of colors, or blend a color and white.

On these pages you need:
Ledger size white paper
Ledger size piece of cardboard
Medium-thickness soft brush
Things to draw around
Scissors and glue stick
Self-adhesive plastic
Pencil and ruler
Paint

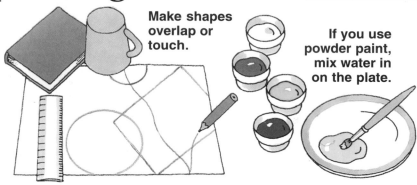

Make shapes overlap or touch.

If you use powder paint, mix water in on the plate.

Draw around things to make shapes on the paper. Draw your own shapes too. Do about six shapes altogether.

Prepare yellow, red, blue and white paint. Choose two colors to blend. Put a little of one on a plate.

Blend each new color into the last one.

Paint one end of a shape. Add the second color to the first, little by little. Fill more of the shape each time.

Remember to wash the brush in clean water.

Paint another shape with a different color blend. You could paint in a different direction this time.

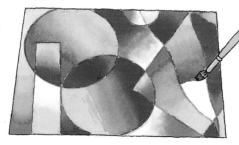

Fill each shape with a blend. Work carefully, until the whole picture is full of blended color.

Multi-color jigsaw

Do a color-blend painting, or go to a photocopying business and get a color copy of your first painting.

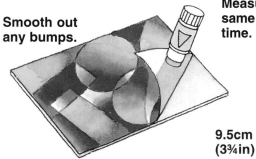

Smooth out any bumps.

Put glue all over the back of the painting. Try not to miss any place. Stick it onto the cardboard. Leave it to dry.

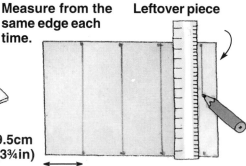

Measure from the same edge each time.

Leftover piece

9.5cm (3¾in)

On the back, mark dots every 9.5cm (3¾in) on the long edges. Join the dots with a pencil and ruler.

Bookmarks

Do a smaller painting. Glue it to cardboard and cut it into strips. Cover each one with self-adhesive plastic.

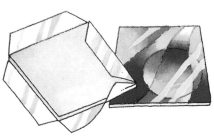

Can you spot where the shapes and color blends match up?

See if your friends can do your jigsaw.

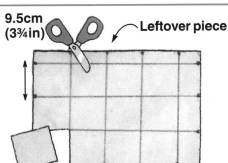

9.5cm (3¾in) → **Leftover piece**

Mark dots every 9.5cm (3¾in) along the short edges and join the dots. Then cut the squares out carefully.

Smooth out bubbles.

Make the plastic square bigger than the painted one.

Cut a square of self-adhesive plastic. Peel off the backing. Lay the plastic on the front of a jigsaw piece.

Snip the corners off the plastic. Fold the edges over and smooth out any bumps. Cover all the squares.

Thick paint

You can use paint thickly, so that it looks and feels bumpy, or "textured" when it dries. Paint used like this is called "impasto".

On these pages you need:
Paints and white glue*
A sketchbook or letter size paper
Ledger size sheet of paper
Thin, soft brush and a stiff brush
Flour, rice and a teaspoon
Pencil, ruler, round-ended knife
Scissors and a glue stick
Colored cardboard

Experiments

Draw squares on the paper or sketchbook. Put the paint in pots. Mix a teaspoonful of glue into each one.

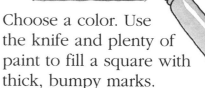

Choose a color. Use the knife and plenty of paint to fill a square with thick, bumpy marks.

Thick paint frieze

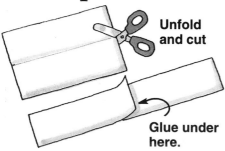

Unfold and cut

Glue under here.

Fold the ledger size paper in half lengthways. Unfold it and cut along the crease. Glue two short edges together.

Mix a pale, runny color. Use a thin brush to paint a simple scene. Just paint the outlines of the shapes.

Mix plenty of paint on a plate before you add anything to it.

Clean tools before the paint dries on.

Decide which part to fill in first. Mix a color you like. Choose one of the ways of painting you tried above.

Paint color onto another square with a stiff brush. Scrape into it with the wooden end of the brush.

Mix a little rice into one color and flour into another. Paint these onto squares with a knife.

Textured cards

Make more textured squares and let them dry. Fold a rectangle of cardboard in half. Cut out the squares and glue some on the card in a pattern.

You could make lots of cards in different sizes.

Scrape into the paint before it dries.

You could try painting a second color onto pieces that are wet.

Use colors that look good together.

Now paint another part in a different way. If you scrape into wet paint, paint and scrape a little at a time.

Paint each part of the picture in a new way. When it is dry, feel the bumpy patterns.

Color-match spirals

Mixing colors to match ones you can see is an important skill. You can practice it when you make the spirals on these pages.

On these pages you need:

Scraps of colored paper
from magazines
A sketchbook or letter size paper
Pencil, scissors and a glue stick
Big sheet of thin white cardboard
Strips of white paper
Paints and soft brushes
Needle and thread

**Make piles
of colors.**

Tear colors from the scrap paper. Glue colors that look nice together in your sketchbook, in a trail.

Draw a big spiral on the cardboard. Start in the middle and draw around and around four or five times.

If you use powder paint see page 38 for mixing reminders.

Draw lines in different places on the spiral, to make lots of sections. Prepare your paints, too.

Medium-thickness brush

See pages 38 and 39 for reminders about making colors.

Which colors do you need for making the first one in your paper trail? Mix small amounts on a plate.

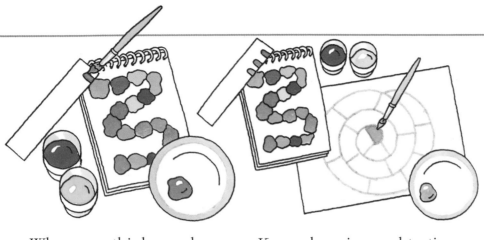

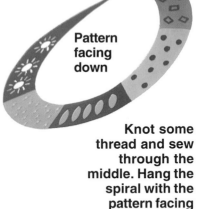

When you think you have made the color, paint a blob on a paper strip. Does it match the scrap?

Keep changing and testing the color to get the best match you can. Then paint the middle of the spiral.

Pattern facing down

Knot some thread and sew through the middle. Hang the spiral with the pattern facing down or up.

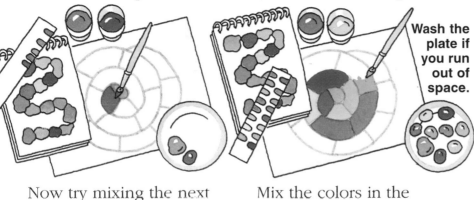

Wash the plate if you run out of space.

Now try mixing the next color in the paper trail. Then paint the next section in your spiral.

Mix the colors in the paper trail one at a time. Each time you match a color, paint it in the spiral.

Hang your spiral from the ceiling or a door frame.

Pattern facing up

Thin brush

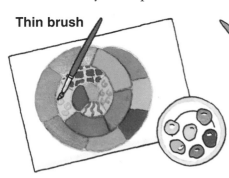

Thick brush

Color for back

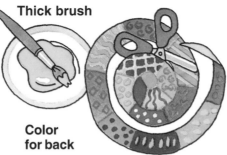

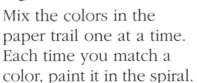

Make more spirals. Hang them on one thread.

When the spiral is dry, paint a pattern on each shape. Mix a new color for each pattern.

Paint the back one color and let it dry. Turn it over and cut out the spiral along the curling line.

You could decorate both sides of your spirals.

Look, paint and print

To paint something you can see, look very carefully. Make the shapes and colors as accurate as you can.

On these pages you need:
An orange cut in half around the middle, on a saucer
A sketchbook or white paper
A strip of white paper
Paints, brushes and scissors
A glue stick and adhesive tape
String and thick cardboard
Big sheets of white and colored paper

1

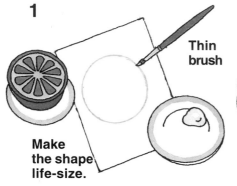

Thin brush

Make the shape life-size.

Mix a runny, light color on the plate. Look at the cut surface of the orange. Paint the shape of the outline.

2

Spaces between shapes

Skin

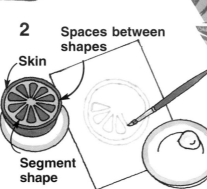

Segment shape

Paint lines to show the shapes you can see inside the orange. Can you see the things shown above?

3

Try different yellows or reds if you have them.

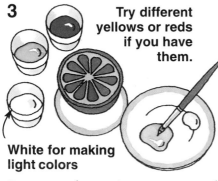

White for making light colors

Prepare the paints you need to make the colors in the orange. Then try mixing the lightest color you can see.

4

Look carefully to check which are the light parts.

Test the color on a paper strip. When it matches the orange's light parts, paint those parts on your picture.

5

Mix and test the color you need for the segments, then paint them. Do you need another color for the skin?

Fruity wrapping paper

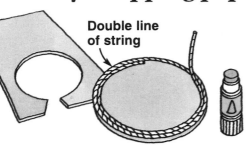

Double line of string

Draw the shape of the orange on cardboard and cut it out. Glue a double line of string around the edge.

Cut out another shape the same size. Draw segments on it and cut them out. Glue them onto the first shape.

Cut a strip of cardboard. Fold it in half, then fold the ends outward. Tape it to the back of the shape.

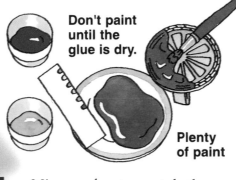

Don't paint until the glue is dry.

Plenty of paint

Press all over the shape.

Paint the shape again for each new print.

Mix a color to match the segments in your painting. Paint it onto the printing block with a thick brush.

Press the block firmly onto a big sheet of paper, then take it off. Cover the whole sheet like this.

Print an orange and cut it out to make a gift tag.

Print a small piece of paper if you are wrapping a small present.

Overlap shapes. You could use a second color.

Try printing onto different colors.

Still life

A painting or drawing of a collection of things is called a still life. Here you can find out how to try to paint a still life yourself.

On these pages you need:
Letter size paper or bigger (colored or white)
A strip of paper the same color as the paper you paint on (for testing colors)
Thick and thin brushes
Paints
A collection of objects

Setting up

First, choose some things you would like to paint. Then find a place where you can arrange them and leave them. Start to place things together. Move them, add things or take them away until they look nice.

Try to have different colors in your arrangement.

You could use some patterned paper or cloth for extra interest.

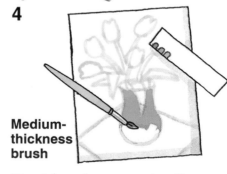

Choose things which are interesting shapes.

Painting

1

Decide which way up to have the paper. Which way suits the arrangement best? Then mix a pale color.

2

Use a thin brush to paint the shapes you see. Start with the outlines of the big, main shapes.

3

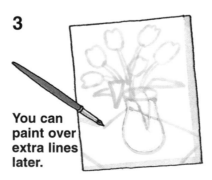

You can paint over extra lines later.

Then paint the shapes of smaller things. It may help to paint in lines where things overlap.

4

Medium-thickness brush

Decide what to paint first. Mix the main color and test it on the paper strip, next to the real thing.

50

5

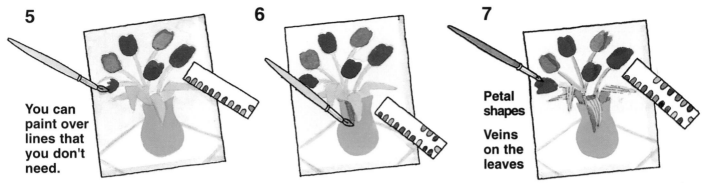

You can paint over lines that you don't need.

When the paint dries, fill in more shapes. Test each color you mix before you use it. Add a background.

6

Can you see any shadows? Mix darker tones to paint these pieces. Mix lighter tones for light pieces.

7

Petal shapes

Veins on the leaves

When the paint is dry, look for shapes and details on the thing you are painting. Paint these in too.

8

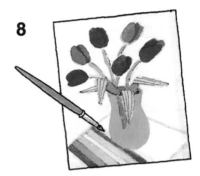

If any of the things have patterns on them, add these last. A thin brush is best for delicate patterns.

Extra tips

Look at the things you are painting again and again while you work.

Mistakes don't matter. Just paint over them when the paint dries.

Leave your painting and come back to it, to see if you need to do more.

Painting people

A portrait can be drawn or painted. Ask someone to be your model, so you can paint their portrait. Make it as much 1ike them as you can. Or look in a mirror and paint a self-portrait instead.

On these pages you need:
Ledger size paper (colored or white)
A strip of paper the same color that you paint on
Letter size paper
Different thickness brushes
Paints
A mirror you can hold
A glue stick and colorful scraps of paper

Mini paintings

Make small paintings of your own eyes, nose and mouth by looking in the mirror, to get used to the shapes.

Use a runny color.

The portrait

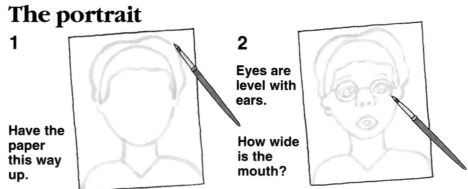

1

Have the paper this way up.

Mix a pale, runny color. Paint the shape of your model's head, hair and shoulders. Use a thin brush.

2

Eyes are level with ears.

How wide is the mouth?

Look carefully at the eyes, ears, nose and mouth. Paint the shapes in. If your model has glasses, add these too.

3

Mix a color to match the skin. This can be tricky, so keep testing it. Paint the skin with a medium brush.

4

Can you see shadows around the nose, mouth and chin? If so, mix a darker tone and paint in these parts.

5

Mix a color to match the hair. Paint it to show which way it grows. Is it straight or curly? Does it stick out?

6

Mix the colors you need to paint the eyes. Paint them in with a thin brush. Paint the mouth and eyebrows too.

7

Paint your model's clothes. Can you copy the colors or patterns? Paint details like jewelry or glasses too.

8

Paint a colored background with a thick brush, or do a pattern. Paint around the portrait very carefully.

More ideas

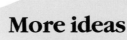

Make a little self-portrait with a thin brush. Get some copies made at a copy store. Cut them out and glue them at the top of notepaper when you write to friends.

Glue colored scraps of paper onto a portrait to make colorful clothes.

53

Sponge and spatter

You can make colorful patterns by sponging or spattering paint onto paper.

On these pages you need:

Ledger size white paper
Paints and a pencil
Paintbrush for mixing
A small sponge
An old toothbrush
Scissors and a ruler
Mounting putty
A big piece of scrap cardboard
Newspaper and adhesive tape

Starry paper

1

Draw a star on cardboard. Cut it out. Draw around it lots of times to cover all the cardboard with stars.

2

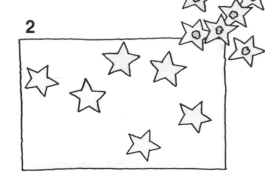

Cut out the stars. Put a blob of mounting putty on each one. Press half of them gently onto the white paper.

3

Hold the star as you dab.

Blotchy marks look good.

Choose two colors. Mix plenty of the lightest one on a plate. Dip the sponge in. Dab around the stars.

4 Clean the plate first.

When the paint is dry, place the other stars in the spaces. Mix and sponge on the other color.

5

When the paint is dry, peel the stars off very carefully. See the bright pattern appear piece by piece.

Spattering

Spread lots of newspaper first.

Dip the toothbrush in the paint. Hold it over the paper and pull your finger along the bristles. Do this again and again.

Spattered paint looks more delicate than sponged paint.

54

More ideas

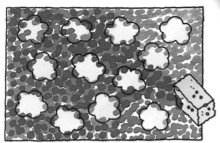

Position all the shapes at once. Sponge on the first color. Sponge another color lightly over the top.

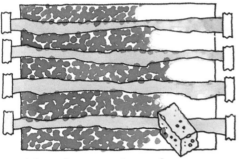

Tear long strips of paper or newspaper. Lay them across the paper and tape them down. Sponge on color.

You could paint extra detail on top of shapes with a thin brush.

Think of different shapes you could use.

Stripes could go from top to bottom, from side to side or both.

Book covers

Open the book. Lay it on the bottom edge of some big patterned paper. Draw a line where the top comes to.

Cut off the extra piece at the top. Then fold the side pieces over the cover and press firmly along the folds.

Painting outdoors

To paint outdoors, take everything you need with you. The best way to do this is to make a painting kit. Take it on vacation, to a friend's house or into the park or backyard.

On these pages you need:

A small sketchbook or eight sheets of letter size paper (white and colored)
Pencil, ruler, thick needle, thread and scissors
Strong shoe box, long cardboard tube, elastic bands
Paints and five little plastic pots with lids
Brushes and a rag (or kitchen paper towel)
Two circles of material (about 12cm (3¾in) across)
Screw-top jar that fits in the box when the lid is on
Small plastic plate or lid of a plastic container

Homemade sketchbook

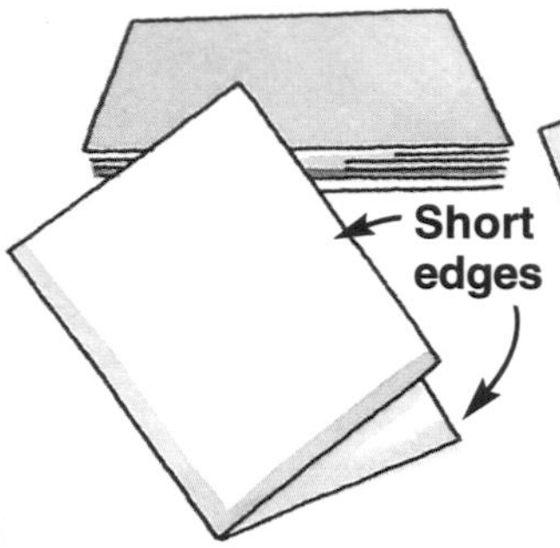

Short edges

7cm (2¾in)

14cm (5½in)

Fold eight sheets of paper in half, or cut bigger paper to letter size then fold it.

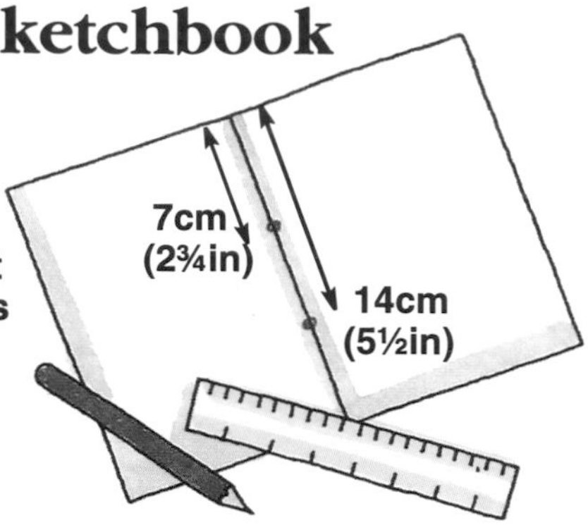

On each piece, mark dots 7cm (2¾in) and 14cm (5½in) along the fold.

Take a pencil for making notes.

Take a small sketchbook or make one yourself. Find out how above.

Paintbrushes go in this tube. Secure a circle of material over each end with an elastic band.

You may need to cut the end off the tube, so it fits in the box.

Take a rag or paper towel to dry brushes on.

Half fill each pot with paint. Put the lids on firmly.

Use a small plastic plate or the lid of a plastic container for mixing colors on.

Half fill the jar with water. Screw the lid on tightly.

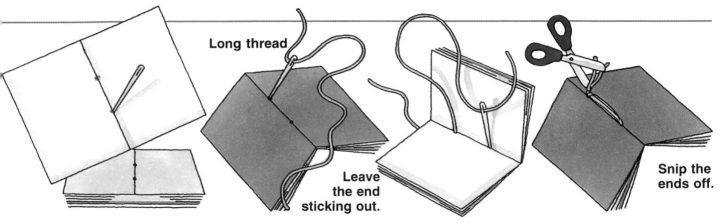

Long thread

Leave the end sticking out.

Snip the ends off.

Use the thick needle to make holes where the dots are. Or ask an adult to help you.

Thread the needle. Poke it through the first hole while you hold all the paper.

Turn the paper over. Poke the needle down through the other hole.

Sew through the holes four times. Unthread the needle. Tie a double knot.

Things to paint

Here are some ideas for things you could paint. Can you think of some more?

You could paint over two whole pages.

Make a picture diary of things you see and do each day on vacation. You could write notes, too.

Paint flowers and insects in the yard.

Tips for using your kit

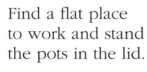

Use a ribbon or a big elastic band to hold the lid on the box.

Find a flat place to work and stand the pots in the lid.

Clean everything in your kit afterward, ready for next time.

Paint and stick

You can make a collage by gluing on pieces of paper. Use collage and paint together, to make an imaginary jungle picture.

On these pages you need:
A big sheet of colored paper (ledger or bigger), or white paper painted with a blue or gray blended background
Paints, brushes, scissors, glue
An extra sheet of paper
Scraps of colored paper
Bowls (about seven)

1

Look in books for ideas.

Leave space for lots of other things.

Paint an animal on the big paper. It could be a tiger or another wild animal, or you could make up your own.

2

You need big and small pieces.

Tear lots of different colors from your collection of scrap paper. Put a color group in each bowl.

3

Torn edges can look good.

How big is your plant going to be?

Decide where to put the first plant. Tear or cut out big leaves from the scrap collection. Glue them on.

4

Do another plant. Make the leaves a different shape this time. You could use a different color, too.

5

Use dark colors for shadows.

Add more plants. Some could hang down. Then paint in the stems and paint veins on the leaves.

6

Paint long grass to hide part of your animal, or glue on paper grass. The animal could be peeping out.

7

Add some bright jungle flowers. Paint them, or make them from colored paper. Do different kinds.

8

Paint colorful butterflies, birds, caterpillars, snakes and other creatures on a new piece of paper.

9

Cut the creatures out and stick them in the jungle. Add as much as you like. You could add more another day.

Jungle pots

Buy a terracotta flower pot from a garden center. Paint it to look like an animal's coat. You could do tiger stripes or leopard spots. Stick on leaves and flowers, then paint more details on top. You could ask an adult to varnish it for you.

Use paint and paper to decorate a collection of jungle pots. Each pot could be different.

Computer paintings

Different art programs let you make pictures on the computer screen. The programs do the same kinds of things. These pages tell you how to make pictures with the Microsoft® Paintbrush™ program which you use with Microsoft® Windows® software.

The display

A display on the computer screen shows you all the things you can use to make a picture.

This is called the Toolbox. You choose which tool to use. (Find out more on page 90).

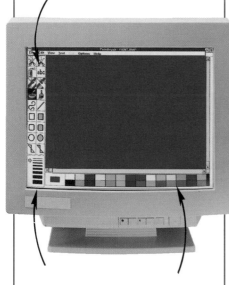

Change the thickness of the mark you make by choosing one of these lines.

This shows the colors you can use. It is called the Palette.

First marks

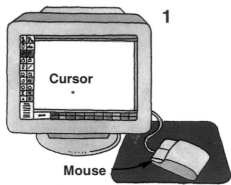

1

Cursor

Mouse

Move the mouse on the pad to move the dot on the screen called the cursor.

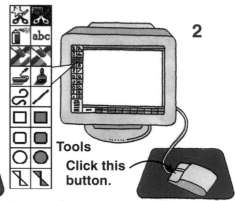

2

Tools

Click this button.

Move the cursor to the brush in the tools section. Click the left mouse button.

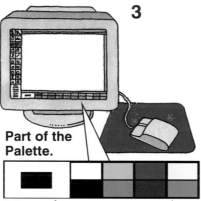

3

Part of the Palette.

Move the cursor to a color. Pick it by clicking the left mouse button.

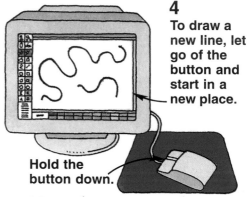

4

To draw a new line, let go of the button and start in a new place.

Hold the button down.

Move the cursor to the middle. Move the mouse as you press its left button.

Draw and fill

Brush tool

Pick the Brush tool, then pick a color. Move the mouse to draw wiggly shapes on the screen.

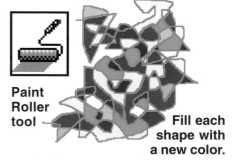

Paint Roller tool

Fill each shape with a new color.

Pick the Paint Roller tool and a color. To fill a shape, move the cursor to it and click the left mouse button.

Brush thickness

Line thicknesses

Paint a picture using lots of different colors and line thicknesses.

Painting ideas

Experiment with more tools. Then make paintings using the skills you have learned. Here are a few ideas.

Stormy sea

Spray paint

Airbrush tool

Pick the Airbrush tool. Use it to spray different colors and patterns.

Ask someone to show you how to save your paintings.

Party time

Amazing plants and flowers

You don't have to make the paintings very realistic.

More ideas

If you have a color printer, print out your favorite paintings. There are businesses which do color photocopies onto T-shirts. You could get one of your paintings copied. This is fairly expensive, but it makes a good present. See how to draw letters on page 90.

Artists and paintings

Everyone has their own way of doing things. Here are some of the different things artists do when they paint.

They stand back to look at their painting. This helps them decide what to do to it next.

They sometimes take a break and do something else instead. Then they do more to the painting.

They paint over parts of the picture and make changes, until they are happy with it.

Some artists take an hour to do a painting. Other artists take weeks, months or even years.

Artists often make more than one painting at a time. They do a little of one, then a little of another.

Some artists paint things on the spot. Others make lots of rough drawings and paintings first. They look at these later, to help them do a finished painting.

Finding paintings

You can see paintings in art galleries or museums. An art gallery is a room or a building where you can see works of art. Most towns have one.

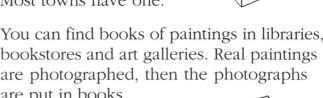

You can find books of paintings in libraries, bookstores and art galleries. Real paintings are photographed, then the photographs are put in books.

You can buy cards and postcards with photographs of paintings on them. Look on the back to find out how big the real thing is and who the artist is.

Looking at paintings

Here are some questions you can ask yourself when you see a painting you like.

> What can I see in the picture?

> How does the painting make me feel?

> Has the artist made the paint look bumpy or smooth?

> Can I see the brush marks?

> Who made the painting and how big is it?

Artists and skills

Here are some artists who used painting skills you have learned in this book. The dates tell you when the artists lived. Can you find any of their paintings to look at?

Jackson Pollock (1912-1956) made his paintings by spattering and dribbling paint. Some of his paintings are enormous.

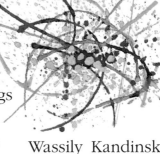

Wassily Kandinsky (1866-1944) made some paintings full of blended color. They had lots of shapes in them.

Vincent van Gogh (1853-1890) used thick, bright paint. His brush marks make swirling patterns. He often took his painting kit out and made paintings on the spot.

Vincent van Gogh also painted portraits. He painted many self-portraits too.

Paul Cézanne (1839-1906) painted lots of still lifes.

More paintings

Here are some more artists whose paintings you could look for. It tells you where you can see some of them, if you live nearby, or visit on holiday.

Salvador Dali (1904-1989)

Dali tried out lots of different styles. He belonged to a group of artists called the Surrealists, whose pictures are somewhat like things you dream. You can see his work in the *Salvador Dali Museum in Figueras, Spain.*

Paul Gaugin (1848-1903)

Gaugin was born in France but did many paintings on a South Sea island called Tahiti. He used bright colors and bold outlines. You can find his work in the *Museum of Fine Arts in Boston, USA, and the Jeu de Paume in Paris.*

Roy Lichtenstein (1923-1997)

He was an American pop artist. He is best known for his paintings of comic strip heroes. His work is mostly in galleries in *New York, USA,* such as the *Guggenheim Museum, Metropolitan Museum of Art and the Museum of Modern Art.*

L. S. Lowry (1887-1976)

Lowry was born in Manchester, England. He is famous for his matchstick men. These are the stick-like people which fill his pictures. He liked to paint crowded streets, chimneys, factories and bridges. You can find the largest collection of Lowry's work in *Salford Art Gallery, in Manchester, England.*

Henri Matisse (1869-1954)

Matisse drew and painted. He is famous for the interesting way he uses colors and lines. You can see Matisse's paintings in *the Hermitage in Leningrad; the Pushkin in Moscow and the Barnes Foundation in Pennyslvania.*

Claude Monet (1840-1926)

Monet belonged to a group of artists in Paris called the Impressionists. He painted landscapes using bright colors and bold brushwork. Monet made lots of paintings of his garden, which you can visit at *Giverny,* in *Normandy, France.* The best collections of his work are in Paris at the *Jeu De Paume and the Orangerie galleries of the Louvre.*

Pablo Picasso (1881-1973)

He had lots of new ideas about art. He used oils, ink, crayons, pencil, charcoal, bronze, sheet metal, plaster, stone and even things pulled out of trashcans. His work can be found in the *Museum of Modern Art, New York; the Picasso Museum, Paris, France and Casón del Buen Retiro, Madrid, Spain.* You can find out about his drawings on page 32.

Henri Rousseau (1844-1910)

He is famous for his bold jungle paintings. He liked to paint trees, tropical plants, trunks, leaves and blades of grass. You can see Rousseau's paintings in many *American museums, the museums in Paris and the National Gallery in London, England.*

Georges Seurat (1859-1891)

Seurat is best known for painting in tiny dots of color. This is called pointillism (see page 4). His pictures seem very still and the people look like statues. Many of Seurat's paintings are in the *Metropolitan Museum, New York and the Art Institute of Chicago, USA.* You can learn about his sketches on page 32.

STARTING
LETTERING

Contents

66 Starting out
68 Highs and lows
70 Feathers and teeth
72 Shapes and patterns
74 Seeing double
76 Straight-line letters
78 Cut it out
80 Grow your name
82 That's torn it
84 Curly whirly letters
86 Eat your name
88 Printing letters
90 Letters on a computer
92 Design an alphabet
94 Looking at letters
96 Index

Starting out

In this part of the book you will find lots of different ways of lettering. On these pages you will find some of the things you can use to do your lettering. There are also some important tips to help you.

Bright pencils

Gold or silver pens

Things you can use

You can do lettering on all kinds of paper. If you use bright paper, test your pen or pencil on it first so that you can see if it will show. You can buy different pencils, pens and crayons from art stores and stationary departments.

Thick felt-tip pens

Thin felt-tip pens

Paintbrush

For some of the projects you will also need things like a pair of scissors, a ruler and an eraser.

If you don't have the same type of pen that is used for a project in this book, just use another one.

Left-handers

If you are left-handed, lay the side of your hand on the paper as you write.

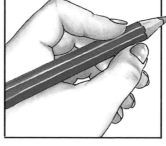

Hold your pencil so that your hand is below, and a little to the left, of your writing.

Hold your pencil with your fingers 2-3cm (¾ -1¼ in) away from the point, like they are in the picture.

Lay your paper so that the left-hand corner is higher than the right-hand corner.

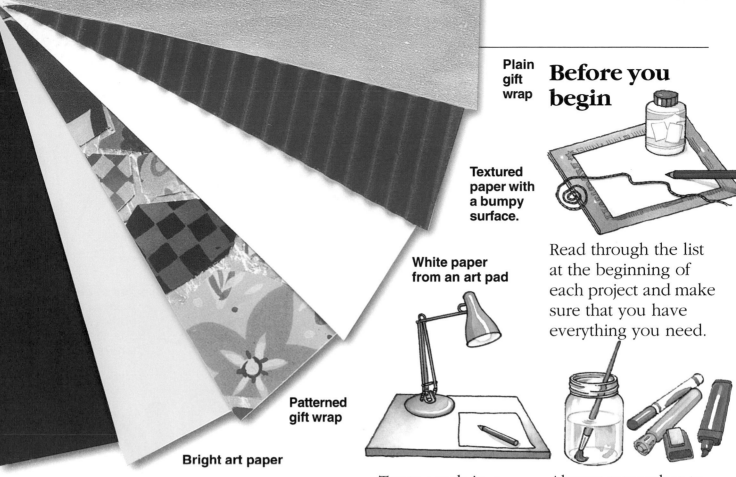

Plain gift wrap

Textured paper with a bumpy surface.

White paper from an art pad

Patterned gift wrap

Bright art paper

It is difficult to write on shiny paper. Use it for letters which you cut out or glue letters onto it.

Before you begin

Read through the list at the beginning of each project and make sure that you have everything you need.

Try to work in a bright place so that your hand doesn't make shadows on your letters.

Always remember to put the lid back on a pen when you have used it. Wash any brushes you use.

Right-handers

Hold your pencil between your thumb and first two fingers, about 1½cm (½in) from the point.

Your hand should be below, and a little to the right, of your writing. Lay the paper as it is in the picture.

Rest the pencil in the V-shape between your thumb and your first finger.

Highs and lows

Letters are made up of different lines and shapes. Some letters are small and round and others are tall. When you begin lettering try to keep your letters even. You can do this by writing between lines.

> **On these pages you will need:**
> A pencil, a ruler and an eraser
> Different shades of paper
> Bright felt-tip pens or pencils
> A large plate

Capital letters fill the top two lines only.

You can change the shape of capital letters by making them thin or wide.

You could add a dot at the end of every line of your letters.

When you draw letters like these (see below), don't make the letters too close together when you begin.

Starting out

Write small letters between these lines.

Make these parts touch the middle lines.

With a pencil and ruler draw four lines the same distance apart. Write some small letters.

Make all tall letters apart from 't' touch the line at the top. Make 't' a little shorter.

Letters like g, p and y have a 'tail' which hangs down. Make the tails touch the bottom line.

Start a word with a capital letter or use all capitals, but don't put a capital in the middle of a word.

Around and around

1

2

Draw a letter with one pen. Choose another one and draw around the outside of the letter.

Choose a third pen and go around the second outline. Keep on going using different pens.

68

Wavy letters

1

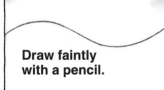

Draw faintly with a pencil.

Draw a wavy line across your paper. Make it wiggle like a snake but don't make the curves too steep.

2

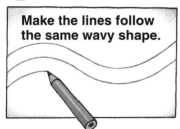

Make the lines follow the same wavy shape.

Draw another wavy line about 1cm (½in) below the first one. Add another line above and below.

3

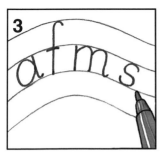

Write a wavy message between the lines. Make capital letters and tall letters fill the top two spaces.

Around the bend

1

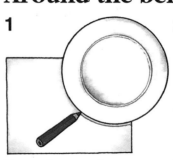

Put a large plate on your paper so that it overlaps one corner. Draw around it faintly with a pencil.

2

Pull the plate out a little and draw around it again. The space between the lines gets narrower at the ends.

3

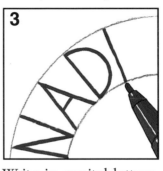

Write in capital letters. Turn your paper as you write so that your letters stand upright between the lines.

Make your letters touch both lines.

Erase your pencil lines when the ink is dry.

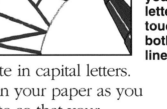

Feathers and teeth

You can join some letter shapes together to make patterns. These patterns can also be used to draw snakes and insects or decorate other animals.

You will need:
Lined paper
White or bright paper
Felt-tip pens
A pencil

Joining up

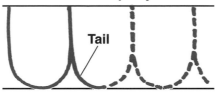

The dotted lines show the shapes you make.

Tail

Use lined paper.

Start with a 'u' shape. Give it a curved tail. Take the tail up to the top line and write another letter 'u'.

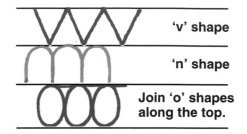

'v' shape

'n' shape

Join 'o' shapes along the top.

Try some other letter shapes. As you write, try not to take your pencil off the paper.

Creepy crawlies

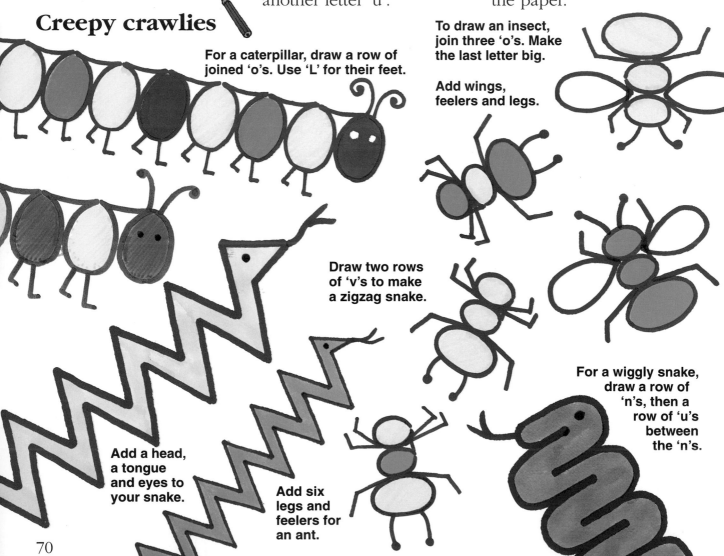

For a caterpillar, draw a row of joined 'o's. Use 'L' for their feet.

To draw an insect, join three 'o's. Make the last letter big.

Add wings, feelers and legs.

Draw two rows of 'v's to make a zigzag snake.

Add a head, a tongue and eyes to your snake.

Add six legs and feelers for an ant.

For a wiggly snake, draw a row of 'n's, then a row of 'u's between the 'n's.

70

Feathery bird

1

With a felt-tip pen, draw the outline of a very fat bird on your paper. Add eyes, a beak and feet.

2
Use a pencil.

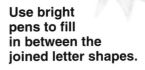

Add lines across its tummy. Make them about two fingers' width apart. Don't worry if they are wobbly.

3

Starting on the left, draw a row of joined letter 'u's between the lines. Try to make them all the same.

4

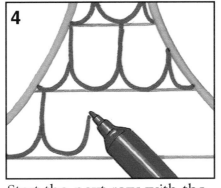

Start the next row with the top of each letter touching the bottom of the one above, as shown.

5

Keep on adding rows until you have filled the tummy. Then erase your pencil lines.

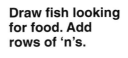

Use bright pens to fill in between the joined letter shapes.

Draw fish looking for food. Add rows of 'n's.

Draw or paint a crocodile with an open mouth.

Add a row of joined 'V's for spiky teeth.

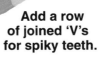

Shapes and patterns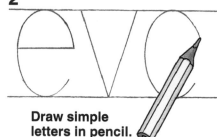

Here are some easy ways that you can make simple letters look more interesting. Before you try any of these letters, always draw faint letters in pencil as a guide (see right).

You will need:
A pencil
Pieces of paper
Felt-tip pens
An eraser
A ruler

Letter guides

1

The lines will help you to keep your letters about the same size.

Use a pencil and a ruler to draw lines which are the same distance apart all the way along.

2

Draw simple letters in pencil.

Write your letters faintly. Make them touch both of the lines and leave small spaces between them.

Use one pen to draw the outline and fill it in with another one.

Fat letters

1

Make any middle part very small.

Round end

Draw an outline around the first letter. Make the ends of the letter very round. This helps to make it look fat.

2

Erase this line.

To make the next letter lie under the first one, overlap their outlines. Erase any lines inside the first letter.

3

Add the other letters in the same way. Go over the outlines with a felt-tip pen. Erase all the pencil lines.

72

Block letters

1

Use capital letters and give them square corners.

Write your letter guides at least a finger-width apart. Draw wide, chunky outlines around the guides.

2

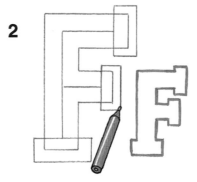

Add a block shape at the ends of the letter shape. Go over the outlines with a pen. Erase the pencil lines.

No outline

Use a pen with a wide tip.

Draw a letter outline in pencil. Add diagonal stripes across it with a pen, then erase all the pencil lines.

Wiggly shapes added with a 'magic' pen (see below).

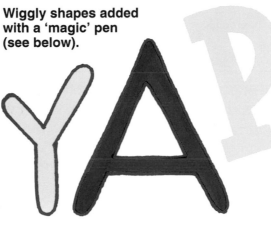

Getting bigger

1

Use a ruler and pencil.

Draw a line across your paper close to the bottom. Add another line like this, joining them at one end.

2

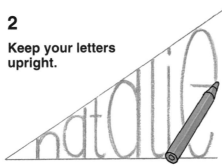

Keep your letters upright.

Write your letters between these lines. Make each one touch both lines. Your letters will get bigger and bigger.

'Magic' change pens

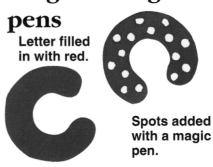

Letter filled in with red.

Spots added with a magic pen.

Try using pens which change from red to yellow, for example, when you go over them with a 'magic' pen.

73

Seeing double

Try lettering with two pencils or pens which are joined together.

You will need:
Adhesive tape
Scissors
Two sharp pencils
Felt-tip pens
Paper

Right hand taping

If you write with your right hand, tape the pencils together like this.

The points should be like this.

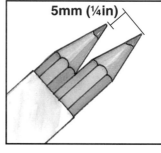

If you are right-handed, hold the pencils with the points level. Tape them together in two places.

Hold the pencils in your right hand as you would normally hold just one pencil on its own.

Left hand taping

5mm (¼in)

Hold the points like this.

If you are left-handed, tape the pencils with the point of the top one 5mm (¼in) below the bottom one.

Hold the pencils as you would normally hold just one. Look carefully to see how to have the points.

Double letters

1

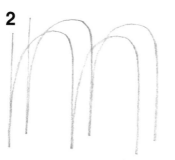

Try to keep the pencil points at the same angle.

It may feel a little odd when you write with two pencils. Begin by making patterns and shapes.

2

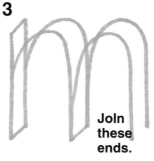

Make the letter big.

Write a letter. Don't turn your wrist as you do it. Can you see thick and thin spaces between the lines?

3

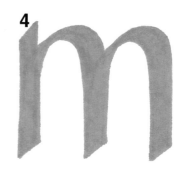

Join these ends.

Use a felt-tip pen to draw over all the lines you have made. Join up the ends of the letters.

4

Fill in the spaces between the lines. Your letters will have some lines which are thicker than others.

You can make 'see-through' letters if you don't fill in between the double lines. Don't forget to join the ends of the lines.

Make a pen

You can make a thick double-tip felt pen from cardboard.

Fill in part of a pattern and try small letters.

Try some of the letter patterns on page 70.

You will need:
Thick cardboard
15x2cm (6x¾in)
A strip of felt
10x2cm (4x¾in)
Scissors
A rubber band
Ink or food dye
An old saucer

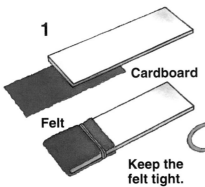

1

Cardboard

Felt

Keep the felt tight.

Lay the cardboard halfway along the felt, then fold the felt over. Fasten it with a rubber band.

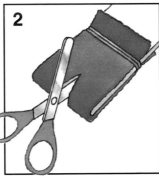

2

Snip a V shape through the felt and the cardboard at the end. Try to make it in the middle.

3

Hold it like your double pencils.

Put a little ink or runny food dye on a saucer. Dip the tip of your 'pen' into it and write big letters.

Join the ends of a dot.

75

Straight-line letters

Although some letters, such as s, b and p have curvy parts, you can make every letter using straight lines only.

You'll be left with white spaces where the tape had been.

Masking tape letters

1

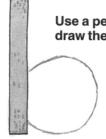

Use a pencil to draw the letter.

Draw a large letter on paper. Cut some tape to fit over the line where you started your letter. Press it down.

2

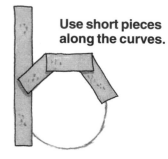

Use short pieces along the curves.

Add another piece of tape. Overlap the first one a little. Add more tape until you finish your letter.

Letter on a plate

1

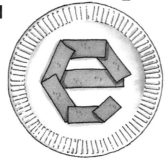

Draw a big letter in the middle of the plate. Cut strips of masking tape to cover the lines.

2

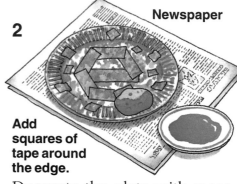

Newspaper

Add squares of tape around the edge.

Decorate the plate with more tape. Pour some paint onto a saucer. Dip the sponge into it then dab all over.

3

Erase all the pencil lines.

When the paint is dry, sponge on a different one in patches. When all the paint has dried, peel off the tape.

Candle letters

1

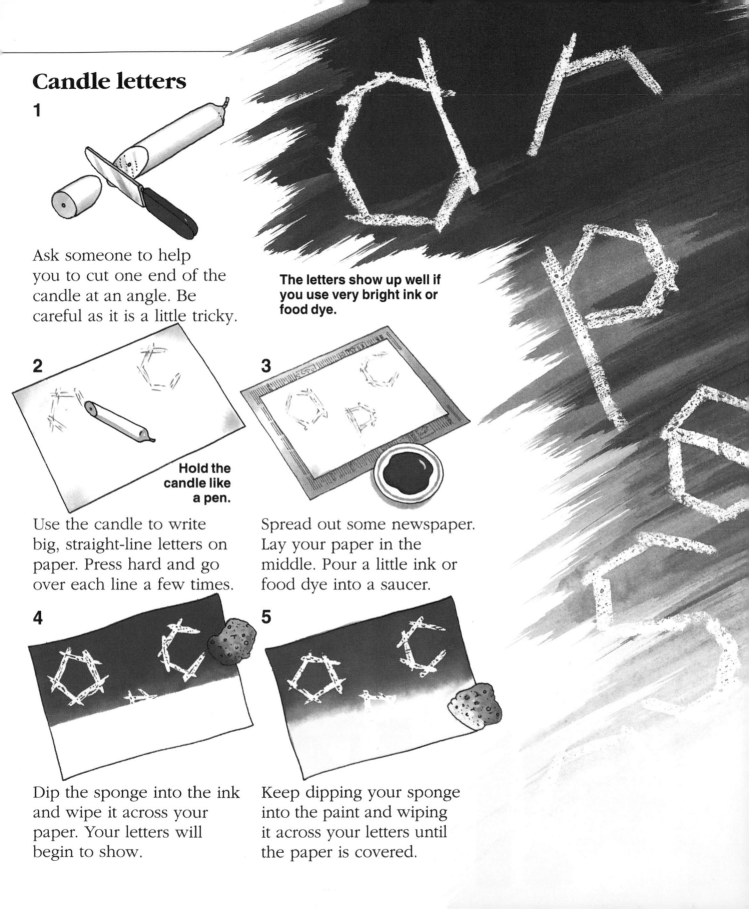

Ask someone to help you to cut one end of the candle at an angle. Be careful as it is a little tricky.

The letters show up well if you use very bright ink or food dye.

2

Hold the candle like a pen.

Use the candle to write big, straight-line letters on paper. Press hard and go over each line a few times.

3

Spread out some newspaper. Lay your paper in the middle. Pour a little ink or food dye into a saucer.

4

Dip the sponge into the ink and wipe it across your paper. Your letters will begin to show.

5

Keep dipping your sponge into the paint and wiping it across your letters until the paper is covered.

Cut it out

Another way to make letters is to cut them out, instead of writing them. You can use these letters in all kinds of ways, such as for making cards or gluing them onto project folders.

You will need:
Different types of bright paper, gift wrap or cardboard with a bumpy surface
Scissors
A pencil

1

You need to make your letters big and bold.

Draw a faint letter in pencil. Make your letter fatter by adding a straight or curvy outline around it.

Try all kinds of different shapes and styles for your letters.

2

Add any middle parts to your letter.

It's a good idea to cut around your letter roughly and then cut it out neatly.

3

Snip it inside the middle part.

If your letter has a middle part, bend the paper and make a snip. Push the scissor blade in and cut it out.

Letters on a T-shirt

You could use cut-out letters to decorate a T-shirt.

You will need:
Tracing paper
A dark felt-tip pen
Clear self-adhesive plastic
A pale T-shirt
A large piece of cardboard
Fabric paint
A thick paintbrush
Scissors and a pencil
Adhesive tape

1

Draw some very big letters on the tracing paper then draw around their outlines with a felt-tip pen.

You could cut out some shapes as well as letters.

2

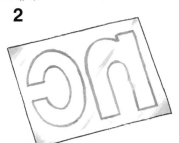

Turn the paper over so that your letters are back to front. They will be the correct way on your T-shirt.

3

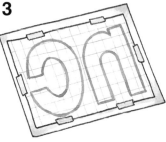

Lay a piece of self-adhesive plastic on top of your letters, with the shiny side down. Tape it on.

4

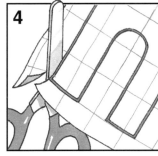

Use a pencil to trace your letters. Cut around them roughly, then cut them out very neatly.

5

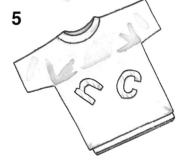

Push the cardboard inside your T-shirt. Peel the backing paper off your letters and press them on.

6

Dip your brush in fabric paint. Put the tip of it near to the edge of a letter and flick the brush out.

7

Keep on flicking the paint around the letters. Peel off all the letters when the paint is dry.

Follow the maker's instructions to 'fix' the paint.

Grow your name

It will only take a few days to grow the letters of your name using cress or mustard seeds.

You will need:
Scrap paper and a pencil
Kitchen sponge cleaning cloth
Scissors
A fine-pointed felt-tip pen
A large dinner plate
Cress or mustard seeds
A clean food tray larger than the sponge cleaning cloth
A metal spatula

1

Put the sponge cleaning cloth onto the scrap paper and use a pencil to draw around it.

2

Draw the letters of your name onto the paper. If your name has many letters, you could just draw your initials.

3

Cut out the letters. Place them on the sponge cloth and draw around them with the felt-tip pen.

4

Cut around the letters. Get someone to help you to cut out the middle pieces if there are any.

The little brown seeds are cress and the round white ones are mustard.

5

Put the letters on the plate and sprinkle them with cress seeds. Don't cover them completely.

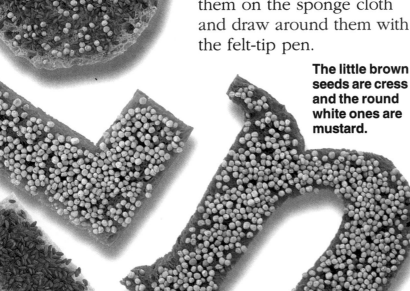

6

Slip a spatula under each letter and lift them onto the tray. Remove any loose seeds with a wet finger.

7 Pour the water onto the tray, not over the seeds.

Put the tray in a warm dark place. Look at it every day and add a little water if the sponge feels dry.

8

After a few days, the seeds start to sprout. Leave the tray on a window sill until the cress grows taller.

You'll see little white roots when the seeds start to sprout.

This letter was covered in mustard seeds.

This is what cress looks like when it grows.

That's torn it

It can be difficult to tear neat letters from paper, but if you brush the paper with water first you'll find it's easy.

1

Brush the outline on thin paper.

Dip your paintbrush into water and draw the outline of a letter. Don't make the letter too small.

2

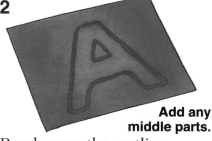

Add any middle parts.

Brush over the outline again then let the water soak into the paper for one or two seconds.

3

Gently push the end of the paintbrush into the paper where you wrote your letter, so that the paper tears.

4

With your fingernail, gently tear around the letter shape. Keep the middle parts you tear out of any letters.

5

Glue on any middle parts in place.

Leave the paper to dry, then glue the back of it. Press it onto another piece of bright paper.

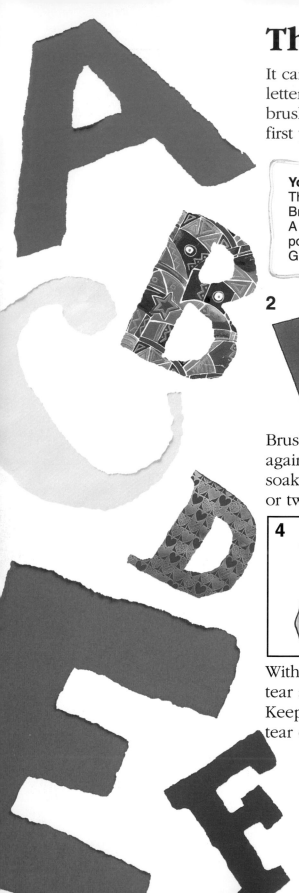

Ripped letter

You can also make bright letters using little pieces of torn paper.

> **You will need:**
> Glue stick
> Bright paper ripped into 1cm (½in) squares
> Piece of thick paper

1

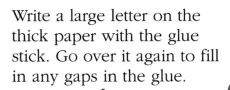

Write a large letter on the thick paper with the glue stick. Go over it again to fill in any gaps in the glue.

If you use shiny paper, draw a back-to-front letter on the back.

2

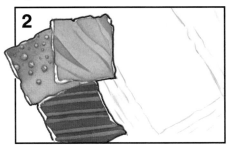

Press a paper square onto the glue at the top of the letter. Press another one on, overlapping their edges.

You could use bright paper from old magazines.

3

Keep on adding squares until the glue is covered. Do it quickly before the glue dries.

The big M was torn out and then another M was torn out carefully inside it.

These letters were glued onto bumpy cardboard. You can buy it in craft stores.

Curly whirly letters

If you bend pieces of string you'll find that you can make really curly letter shapes. You can then use them to do rubbings on paper.

On these pages you will need:
Pieces of thick string
Household glue (PVA)
Scissors
Paintbrush and paints
Paper
Thin cardboard
Wax crayons

If you use bright paper, test your crayon first to make sure that it will show.

1
Make the ends of the letter really curly.

Dip a paintbrush in the glue and draw a large curly letter on a piece of paper. Wash your brush.

2
Use more than one piece of string if you need to.

Before the glue dries, press pieces of string into it. Follow the curved lines you have drawn with the glue.

3

Leave the glue to dry. If you want to paint your letter, mix a little glue with the paint before you use it.

Tip

If your glue is in a bottle with a pointed end, use this to draw your letter instead of using a paintbrush.

Squeeze the bottle to let the glue flow.

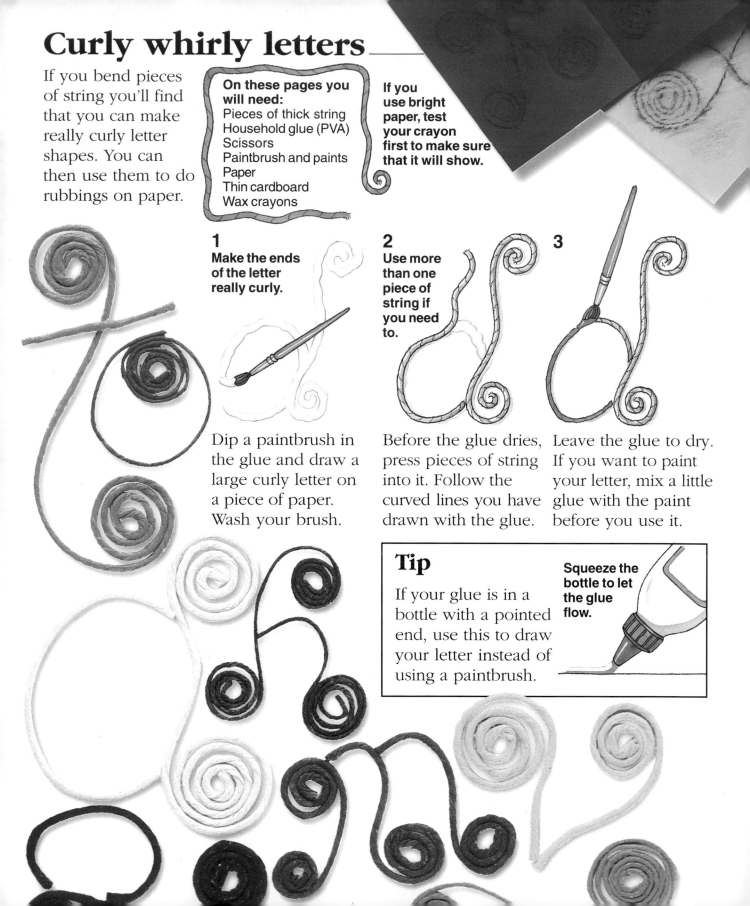

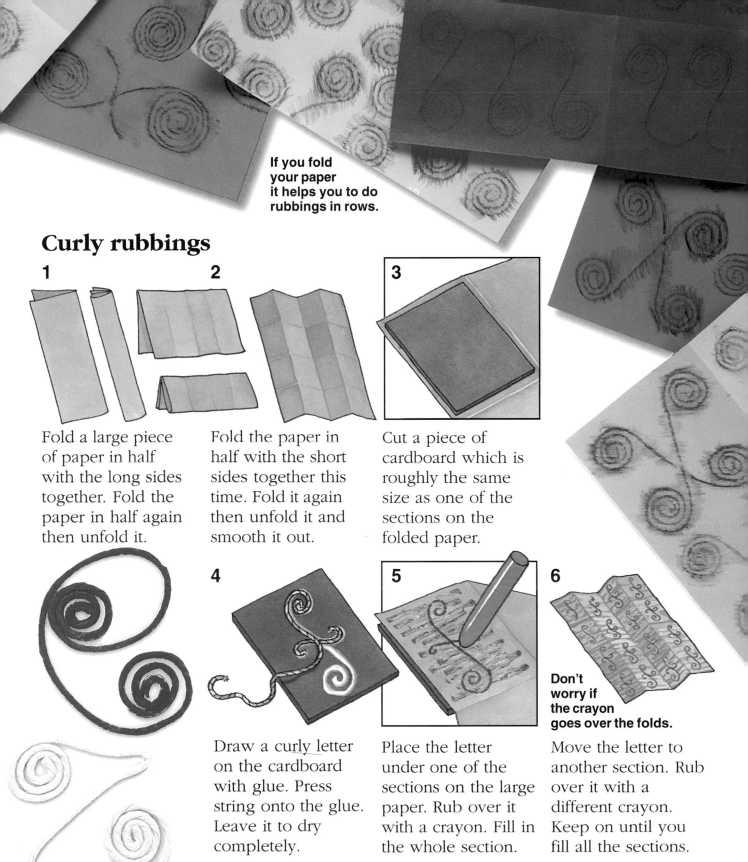

If you fold your paper it helps you to do rubbings in rows.

Curly rubbings

1

Fold a large piece of paper in half with the long sides together. Fold the paper in half again then unfold it.

2

Fold the paper in half with the short sides together this time. Fold it again then unfold it and smooth it out.

3

Cut a piece of cardboard which is roughly the same size as one of the sections on the folded paper.

4

Draw a curly letter on the cardboard with glue. Press string onto the glue. Leave it to dry completely.

5

Place the letter under one of the sections on the large paper. Rub over it with a crayon. Fill in the whole section.

6

Don't worry if the crayon goes over the folds.

Move the letter to another section. Rub over it with a different crayon. Keep on until you fill all the sections.

85

Eat your name

These letters are not only easy to make, you can eat them when you've finished.

Set the oven to 190°C, 375°F, gas mark 5 before you begin.
For about eight letters, you will need:
125g (½ cup) plain flour
50g (¼ cup) margarine
50g (¼ cup) brown sugar
A small egg, beaten
1 teaspoon of ground ginger
A greased baking tray

1

Put the margarine and the sugar together in a big bowl. Mix them until they make a creamy mixture.

2

Sift the flour.

Stir the mixture and add the egg a little at a time. Sift in the flour and the ginger into the bowl.

3

Add a little more flour if the dough feels very sticky.

Stir everything together to make a smooth mixture. Squeeze it with your hands to make a firm dough.

4

Sprinkle some flour on a work surface and place the dough on it. Roll it out until it is about 1cm (½in) thick.

5

Use a blunt knife.

Cut out the letters of your name. If you run out of dough, squeeze the scraps together and roll it again.

6

Slip a spatula under each letter and put it on the greased tray. Bake the letters for about 15 minutes.

7

Ask for help to take the letters out of the oven. Place them on a rack until they are cool.

86

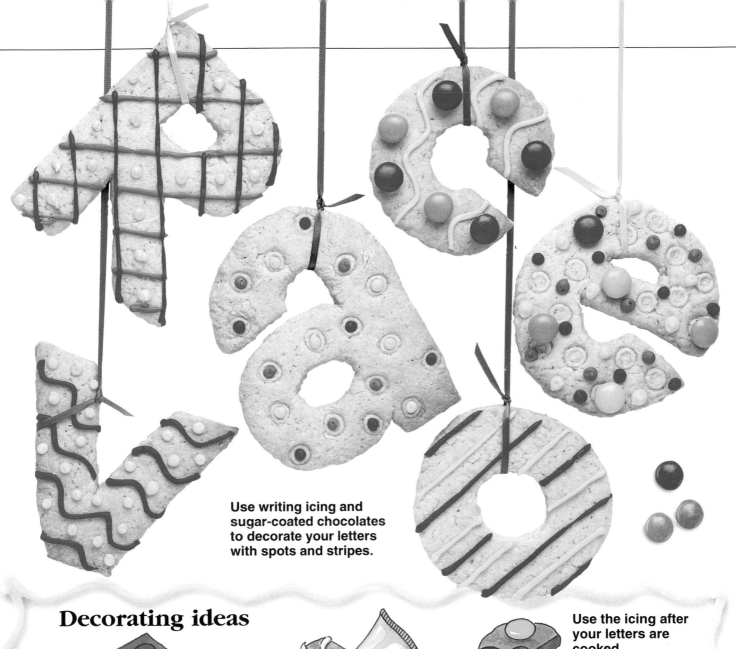

Use writing icing and sugar-coated chocolates to decorate your letters with spots and stripes.

Decorating ideas

Use the icing after your letters are cooked.

To make a spotted letter, press a clean pen top into the dough before you bake your letters.

When your letters have cooled, add lines and spots using writing icing. You can buy this in a supermarket.

Put a spot of icing on the back of a sugar-coated chocolate and then press it on your cooked letter.

Printing letters

Printing is a very quick way of making the same letter again and again.

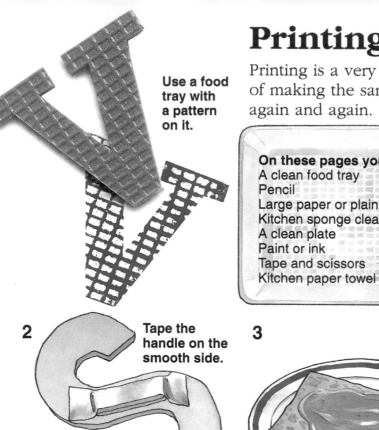

Use a food tray with a pattern on it.

On these pages you will need:
A clean food tray
Pencil
Large paper or plain gift wrap
Kitchen sponge cleaning cloth
A clean plate
Paint or ink
Tape and scissors
Kitchen paper towel

1

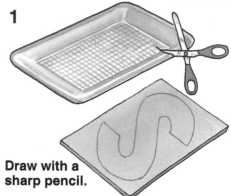

Draw with a sharp pencil.

Carefully cut the bottom off the tray, then draw a letter on the smooth side of it.

2

Tape the handle on the smooth side.

Lay your letter the correct way around.

Cut out your letter. Tape a strip of the tray onto your letter to make a handle.

3

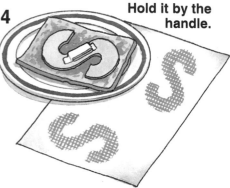

Lay the sponge cloth on the plate and pour some runny paint or ink onto it.

4

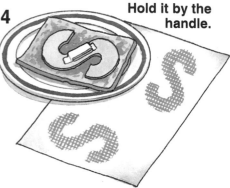

Hold it by the handle.

Push your letter onto the paint on the cloth then press it onto your paper.

The striped letter was printed with bumpy cardboard instead of a food tray.

Use bright gift wrap instead of white paper.

Printed gift wrap

1

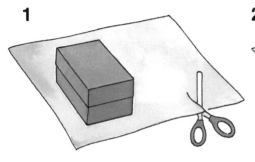

Cut a piece of gift wrap big enough to cover the parcel you are going to cover.

2

Choose paint which will show on the paper.

Start printing at one end. Press your letter in the paint each time you do a print.

3

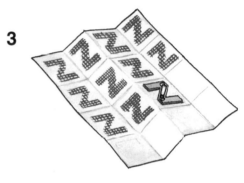

If you print with more than one shade, wipe your letter well before changing paint.

Printing in rows

1

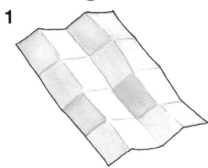

Fold a piece of paper to make sections following steps 1 and 2 on page 85.

2

Cut some food tray slightly smaller than one of the sections. Draw a letter on it.

3

Cut out your letter and print one in each section of the folded paper.

Print an extra letter and glue it onto cardboard to make a gift tag.

Letters on a computer

You can use an art program on a computer to draw your own letters. Most art programs work in a similar way. Here you can find out how to draw letters with the Microsoft® Paintbrush™ program which you use with Microsoft® Windows®.

The Toolbox

You will find the Toolbox running down the left-hand side of your screen. Here are some of the things in the Toolbox which you can use to draw letters.

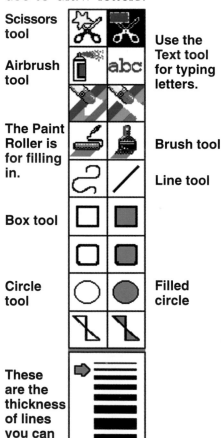

Scissors tool

Airbrush tool

Use the Text tool for typing letters.

The Paint Roller is for filling in.

Brush tool

Line tool

Box tool

Circle tool

Filled circle

These are the thickness of lines you can use.

1

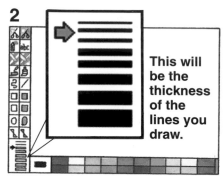

Pick this tool.

Mouse

Move the mouse so that an arrow points to the Brush tool. Click the left-hand button on the mouse.

2

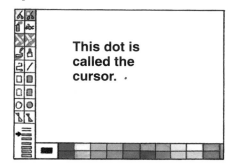

This will be the thickness of the lines you draw.

Choose one of the lines, then click the left-hand button on the mouse. The blue arrow will point to your line.

3

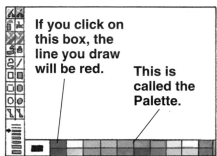

If you click on this box, the line you draw will be red.

This is called the Palette.

Move the arrow to the boxes along the bottom of the screen. Chose one of the boxes and click on it.

4

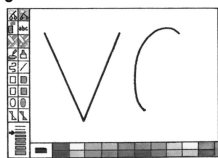

This dot is called the cursor.

Move the mouse so that a dot appears on your screen. Move the dot to the left-hand side of the screen.

5

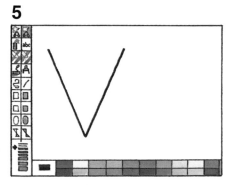

Put your finger on the left-hand button and hold it down. Draw a letter by moving the mouse.

6

To draw another letter, lift your finger off the button, move the mouse and start again in a different place.

Filling in

Draw an outline of a letter on the screen. Make sure the ends of the lines are joined. Draw in any middle parts.

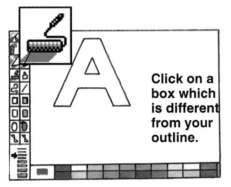

Click on a box which is different from your outline.

Click on the Paint Roller in the Toolbox. Then go down to the Palette at the bottom and click on a new box.

Move the mouse so that the tip of the roller is inside the outline of your letter. Click and your letter will fill in.

Letter ideas

You can draw all kinds of different letters on your computer. The different boxes in the Toolbox give you different shapes and effects. Here are a few for you to try.

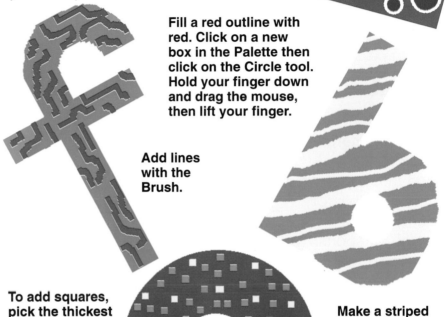

Fill a red outline with red. Click on a new box in the Palette then click on the Circle tool. Hold your finger down and drag the mouse, then lift your finger.

Add lines with the Brush.

To add squares, pick the thickest line. Move the cursor to your letter and click on and off in different places.

Make a striped letter, using some thin and some thick lines.

To get a speckled letter, use the Airbrush tool.

Can you draw an E like this?

Design an alphabet

When you want to design something, you draw it and change it until you are happy with the way it looks. Why not try to design your own picture alphabet?

You will need:
Scrap paper
A pencil
Bright felt-tip pens or pencils

1

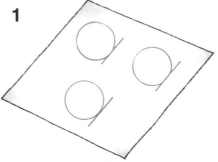

On scrap paper, draw some big letters faintly in pencil. Do the same letter two or three times.

2

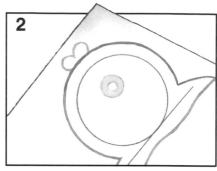

As you draw, think of which shapes you can use to make a round part or a tall straight part of a letter.

Alphabet ideas

Before you begin to design a picture alphabet, it's a good idea to choose a topic for your letters, such as animals or sports. Here are a few letters to give you some ideas.

A snake can bend to make different letters.

You could try to design a whole alphabet of snakes.

A name plate

Once you have designed your alphabet, you could use your new letters to make a name plate for a book or a door.

You will need:
A piece of thin cardboard
Pencils or felt-tip pens
A ruler and an eraser
Scissors
Clear adhesive film
Mounting putty

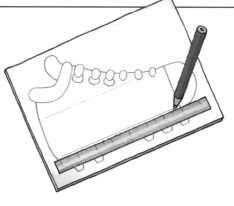

On the cardboard, draw an outline of a big shape. Draw two lines across it using a pencil and a ruler.

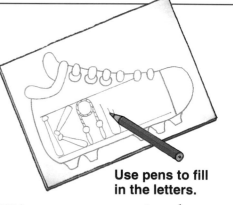

Use pens to fill in the letters.

Write your name using the letters you have designed. Use the lines as a guide for the size of your letters.

3

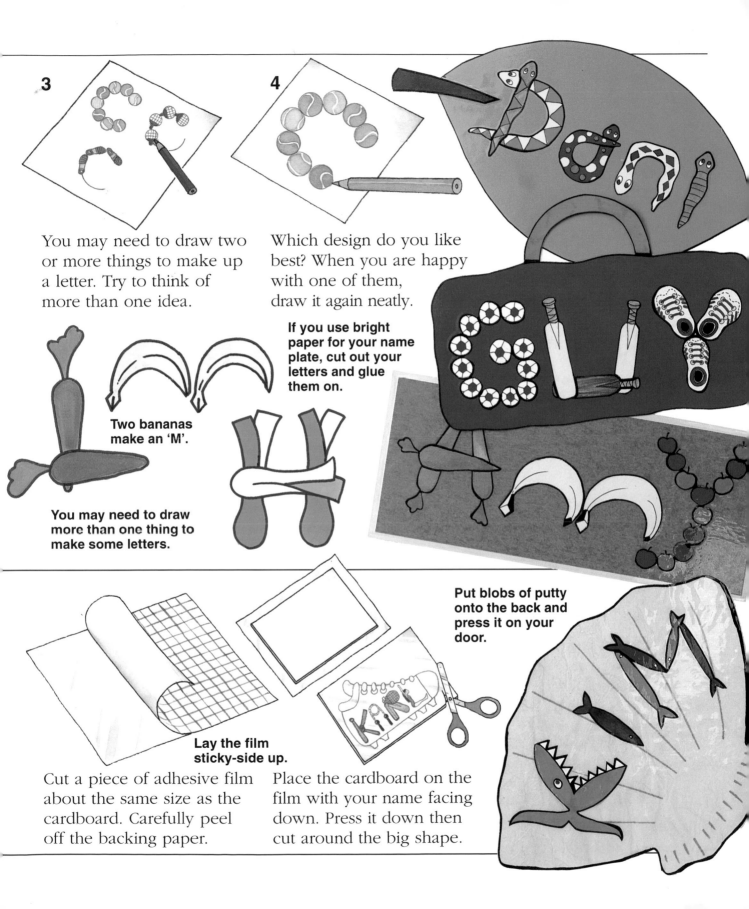

You may need to draw two or more things to make up a letter. Try to think of more than one idea.

Two bananas make an 'M'.

You may need to draw more than one thing to make some letters.

4

Which design do you like best? When you are happy with one of them, draw it again neatly.

If you use bright paper for your name plate, cut out your letters and glue them on.

Put blobs of putty onto the back and press it on your door.

Lay the film sticky-side up.

Cut a piece of adhesive film about the same size as the cardboard. Carefully peel off the backing paper.

Place the cardboard on the film with your name facing down. Press it down then cut around the big shape.

OUT

STOP

Bold letters are used to give information.

Bus station

Looking at letters

Look around you. You can probably see lots of things with letters on them. You'll find all kinds of different lettering on books, comics and magazines, as well as on packets, clothes, posters and television. Look carefully at the letters. Each style has been chosen to suit the thing it is on.

Some lettering looks as if it is making a noise.

CRASH

BOOM

Fireworks

On the beach

Castles

These letters give you an idea of what you might be reading about.

Lettering which catches your eye is used on posters and notices.

Letters in books

The different styles of letters which you see printed in books or magazines are called typefaces. Each typeface was designed by someone and has a name. The typeface you are reading now is called Garamond.
This typeface is called Kids.
This one is called Helvetica.
This one is called Bauhaus.

Serif

F D

Some typefaces have little lines at the ends of the letters. These lines are called serifs.

N S

These are sans serif letters.

Letters which have no little lines are known as 'sans serif'. Can you see any other sans serif letters on this page?

Old lettering styles

If you visit a museum, try to find out if they have any old books or pictures with lettering on them. They may have some old books which have letters decorated with bright paint and real gold.

Letters like this one are called 'illuminated letters'.

Illuminated letters were often used to show where a new chapter started.

All the lettering was drawn and decorated by hand.

An illuminated letter

You could use bright felt-tip pens and a gold pen to draw an illuminated letter. Try to make the style of your letter look old.

You will need:
A pencil and a ruler
White or cream paper
Bright pens
A gold pen

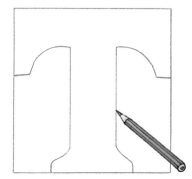

Draw a large box with a pencil and a ruler. Add a letter to fill the box.

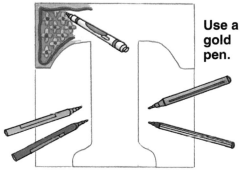

Use a gold pen.

Fill in the letter with tiny patterns. Add some patterns around the letter too.

A lettering book

You could keep a book with different types of lettering in it. Draw your own letters in the book or glue in ones you have written on pieces of paper.

You could also add lettering from old magazines, cards and packets.

Index

abstract drawings, 9
acrylic paints, 34, 36
air drawing, 6, 18
animated pictures, 25
art galleries, 31, 32, 62, 64
artists, 20, 31, 32, 62, 63, 64
    Impressionists, 64
    Surrealists, 64

background, 14
black and white style, 20
blending colors, 40, 41, 42, 43, 63
block letters, 73
brushes, 35

candle letters, 77
capital letters, 68, 69
cartoons, 22, 23, 24, 25, 30
Cézanne, Paul, 63
chalks, 2
charcoal, 3, 64
cleaning up, 37
collage, 7, 20, 32, 58, 59
colors, 34, 64
    blending, 40, 41, 42, 43, 63
    matching, 46, 47
    mixing, 38, 39
    primary, 38, 41
    secondary, 38
computer lettering, 90, 91
computer paintings, 60, 61
Constable, John, 32
crayons, 2, 64, 66
cress letters, 80
cross-hatching, 20
cubes, 12, 13
curly letters, 84, 85
cutting out letters, 78, 79

Dali, Salvador, 64
da Vinci, Leonardo, 31, 32
Degas, Edgar, 32
designing, 28, 29
designing lettering, 92, 93
double letters, 74, 75
double-tip felt pen, 75
drawing outdoors, 30
drawing collections, 32

Escher, M.C., 31

fabric paint, 79
fat letters, 72
features (on faces), 26
felt-tip pens, 2, 66
flick books, 25
foreground, 14, 15

Gaugin, Paul, 64
geometric style, 21
gift wrap, 67, 88, 89
gold pen, 66
growing letters, 80

hatching, 20
highlights, 11
Hockney, David, 32

illuminated letters, 94
illustrations, 30
impasto, 44
Impressionists, 64
ink, 3, 64

joining up, 70, 71

Kandinsky, Wassily, 63
Klee, Paul, 31

landscape paintings, 32, 64
left handers, 66
Leighton, Frederick, 32
letter guides, 72
Lettering book, 95
letters on a T-shirt, 79
letters to eat, 86
letter styles, 94, 95
Lichtenstein, Roy, 64
life drawing, 18, 19, 32
light, 10, 11, 12, 16, 17
line drawings, 32
line paintings, 52
lines, 4, 5, 8, 9, 32, 64
Lowry, L.S., 32, 64

'magic' change pens, 73
masking tape letters, 76
masks, 28, 29
matching colors, 46, 47 50, 51, 52, 53
matchstick men, 64
Matisse, Henri, 31, 64
mixing colors, 38, 39
Monet, Claude, 64
Moore, Henry, 31
mounting, 8, 27
museums, 32, 64

name plate, 92, 93
notebooks, 32

outline, 5, 6, 7, 8, 11, 18, 19, 64

painting kit, 56, 57
paintings, 64
    finding, 62
    looking at, 63

paint,
  colors of, 34
  different kinds of, 34, 36
    thick, 34, 44, 45
paper, 34, 67
pastels, 2, 32
pencils, 2, 10, 64, 66
pens, 32, 66
  double-tip, 75
  felt-tip, 2, 66
  gold, 66
  'magic change', 73
  reed pen, 32
  silverpoint, 32
  stylo tip, 32
Picasso, Pablo, 32, 64
pointillism, 4, 64
Pollock, Jackson, 63
pop art, 64
portraits, 26, 27, 52, 53, 63
postcards, 31
potato printing, 41
powder paint, 34, 36, 38
primary colors, 38, 41
printed gift wrap, 89
printed letters, 88, 89

printing, 41, 49

ready-mixed paint, 34, 36
reed pen, 32
Rembrandt, 32
right-handers, 67
ripped letters, 83
Rousseau, Henri, 64
rubbings, 4, 5, 85

sans serif letters, 94
scratch drawings, 17
secondary colors, 38
self-portraits, 26, 52, 53, 63
serif letters, 94
Seurat, Georges, 32, 64
shading, 10, 11, 12, 13, 19,
  26, 27, 32
shadows, 51, 53, 58
shapes, 6, 7, 8, 9
silverpoint pen, 32
sketchbook, 30, 31, 35, 56, 57
sketches, 31, 32, 64
smudging, 2, 3, 4, 10
spatter painting, 54, 55
speech bubbles, 24

sponging, 54, 55
stained glass style, 20
stand-up mount, 27
still life, 19, 50, 51, 63
string letters, 84
Surrealists, 64
styles, 20, 21, 30, 31, 64
stylo tip pen, 32

tall letters, 68, 69
texture, 4, 7, 44, 45
thickener, 34, 44
thick paint, 34, 44, 45
thought bubbles, 24
tone, 10, 11
torn letters, 82, 83
tracing paper, 14, 15
T-shirt, 79
typefaces, 94

Van Gogh, Vincent, 63

wavy letters, 69

zoom lines, 24

Acknowledgements

Usborne Publishing Ltd. would like to thank the following children for the use of their paintings in *Starting Painting*: Amy Jordan, Kate Squire and Lydia Squire. Thanks also to Catherine Figg for the use of her work. *Starting Drawing*: thanks to Jessica Roberts; *Starting Lettering*: thanks to Rita MacAdam, Elaine Brenchley and Christine Dyer.

Page 60: Microsoft and Windows are registered trademarks, and Paintbrush is a trademark of the Microsoft Corporation.
Photo of ducks on page 14: ©Pal Hermansen/Tony Stone Images.
Pages 90 and 91: Screen shots reprinted with permission from Microsoft Corporation. Microsoft and Windows are registered trademarks of Microsoft Corporation. Paintbrush™ is a trademark of Wordstar Atlanta Technology Center.
Page 95: The illuminated letter at the top of the page, by courtesy of the Board of Trustees of the Victoria and Albert Museum.